THE LAND OF GREEN GINGER

The Land of Green Ginger

NOEL LANGLEY

ILLUSTRATED BY EDWARD ARDIZZONE

faber and faber

First published as *The Tale of the Land of Green Ginger*
by Arthur Barker, 1937

A rewritten version published in Puffin Books 1966

This version first published in Puffin Books 1975

First published in 2001
by Faber and Faber Limited
3 Queen Square, London WC1N 3AU

This edition first published in 2005 by Faber and Faber Ltd

Typeset by AvonDataSet Ltd, Bidford on Avon, Warwickshire
Printed and bound in England by Mackays of Chatham PLC, Chatham,
Kent

A CIP record for this book
is available from the British Library

ISBN 978-0-571-22618-4

10 9 8 7 6 5 4 3 2

Contents

Chapter The First

Which Explains How, Why, When, and Where There Was Ever Any Problem in the First Place

Fortune preserve you, gentle reader. May your days be filled with constant joy, and may my story please you, for it has no other purpose.

And now, if we are all ready to begin, I bring you a tale of the wonderful wandering of an enchanted land which was never in the same place twice.

As long ago as long ago, and as long ago again as that, the City of Peking in Ancient China rang with jubilation, for a son and heir had been born to the Emperor Aladdin.

To commemorate the occasion, the Emperor announced a firework display in the Palace Park, and ordered elegant paper flags in the shape of golden birds to be given to the people of Peking. When these were waved in the crowded streets, the sight was quite enchanting.

On a more serious note, the Grand Vizier summoned a Special Meeting of State to the White Lacquer Room of the Imperial Palace.

You may judge for yourself the importance of this meeting, when I tell you that His Gracious Majesty the Emperor Aladdin presided over it himself. Others present included the Lord Chamberlain; the Prime Minister; two Senior Generals from the Palace Guard; the Master of the Horse; the Mistress of the Robes; and an Unidentified Friend of the Master of the Horse.

'Your Majesty!' began the Grand Vizier imposingly. 'Also Lords and Ladies of the Imperial Court! Also the Friend of the Master of the Horse. We are met here to voice our humble and unworthy joy at the birth of a son and heir to our Celestial Emperor of all the Chinas –'

Here everyone present rose and bowed formally to the Emperor Aladdin, causing him to address them personally.

'Henceforth,' he said considerately, 'you may dispense with the ceremony of rising and bowing at the mention of my name, or we'll never finish this special meeting; and I am naturally anxious not to miss the fireworks which, after all, I paid for. You may proceed, Grand Vizier.'

'Thank you, Your Majesty,' said the Grand Vizier. 'To proceed,' he proceeded, 'you have each been given a piece of paper and a pencil –'

The Lord Chamberlain raised his hand.

'I beg your pardon,' he said politely, 'but by some unpardonable error I have been given no pencil.'

'You have *each* been given,' said the Grand Vizier in a sharper voice, 'a piece of paper and a pencil. On the piece of paper, with the pencil, you will write –'

'No pencil,' said the Lord Chamberlain clearly.

'*On* the piece of paper, *with* the pencil,' said the Grand

Vizier very sharply indeed, 'you will write five names for the Heir Apparent to the Throne. The papers will then be collected and handed to the Emperor, who will decide which name he likes best. A word of caution,' he added gravely. 'I depend on you not to peep at each other's pieces of paper. Anyone found doing this will have his piece of paper torn up, and will not be allowed to watch the fireworks.'

'No pencil,' said the Lord Chamberlain, pathetic now.

The Master of the Horse, who was kinder than some I could mention, broke his pencil in two and gave the Lord Chamberlain the blunt half, and silence fell as everybody present thought very hard, frowning now at the floor, and now at the ceiling, and occasionally at the Emperor Aladdin, though not intentionally; but no one seemed able to think of any names at all, except useless ones like *Tea Pot* and *Bird's Nest Soup*.

Time went by, and the Emperor Aladdin began peering over his shoulder at the window, in case the fireworks started without him. From where he sat he could see all the pieces of paper, and the Lord Chamberlain's was the only one with words on it (and those were crossed out); so at last his impatience got the better of him, and he rose and said with frigid politeness:

[3]

'If it will not disturb your train of thought, I shall excuse myself and retire to the balcony, as I think I hear a bang.'

Everyone present rose and bowed as he departed for the balcony, and the Lord Chamberlain rather forlornly wrote '*Bang*' on his piece of paper, and then thought better of it and drew little faces down the side instead, to help him concentrate.

Out on the balcony, the Emperor Aladdin discovered that hitches and vexations were delaying the fireworks, and he was about to return to the special meeting, when the Queen Mother, the Honourable Widow Twankey, came upon him.

'Ah, *there* you are!' she cried very loudly, seizing him by the sleeve. 'My pearl-encrusted snuffbox, Aladdin! That son of yours! My sapphire tiara! What a child!'

'There's no need to bellow, Mamma,' Aladdin told her kindly. 'We all know how happy you are about it –'

'Happy?' echoed the Widow Twankey. '*Happy?* When your son has just called me; *me*, the Queen Mother; a Button-Nosed Tortoise?'

'Tut! Calm yourself,' Aladdin soothed her. 'A day-old baby doesn't talk!'

'I know it doesn't!' replied the Widow Twankey loudly. 'But he *still* called me a Button-Nosed Tortoise! So don't just *stand* there, Aladdin! *Do* something!'

The Emperor controlled an impulse to say: 'Do what?' or 'Such as?' and proceeded to the Yellow Lacquer Nurseries. There he found his Son and Heir gazing at his foot, which he held against his nose with both hands.

'Hootchie-cootchie, my Itsywitsy!' said the Emperor Aladdin indulgently.

The Son and Heir lowered his foot and gazed up at the Emperor Aladdin.

'And hootchie-cootchie to you too!' he answered good-naturedly.

The Emperor Aladdin opened and shut his mouth in a very dazed manner.

[4]

'*Now* do you believe me?' asked the Widow Twankey with gloomy satisfaction.

The Emperor Aladdin rallied himself and gazed at his Son and Heir with as much dignity as he could muster.

'I understand you called the Queen Mother a Button-Nosed Tortoise?' he inquired.

'That's not quite true,' replied his Son and Heir politely. 'I only said she had a Face like One.'

'He only said you had a Face like One, Mamma,' Aladdin explained weakly.

'And what right had he to say even that?' demanded the Widow Twankey indignantly. 'Even if there *were* such a thing as a Button-Nosed Tortoise; *he* hasn't seen one!'

'True,' agreed the Son and Heir, 'but I'd know him as soon as I saw him!'

'How?' the Widow Twankey challenged him.

'It'd look like you,' said the Son and Heir simply.

'Aladdin! I Refuse to be insulted! *Do* something!' ordered the Widow Twankey angrily.

The Emperor Aladdin looked twice as helpless as he had before.

'Do what?' he asked. 'Such as? I'm completely at a loss! Out of all the thousands and *thousands* of Expectant Fathers in Peking, why did this have to happen to Me?'

'Maybe the stork brought me to the wrong palace?' suggested his Son and Heir apologetically.

'I didn't mean to sound unfatherly,' the Emperor Aladdin floundered kind-heartedly. 'It's just that – it's simply that – what I mean is,' he explained, 'it doesn't *happen*! It's not *possible*! You can't talk at your age! That's all there is to it!'

'Ah, I begin to grasp the problem!' said the Son and Heir, looking suitably pensive. 'It clearly calls for careful thinking on everybody's part.'

'That'll be enough from you!' said the Widow Twankey grimly. 'I can stand Just So Much!'

'The wisest move that I can think of,' said the Emperor Aladdin, 'is to ask Abdul *his* opinion.'

'What? Abdul? Never!' cried the Widow Twankey, awash with fresh alarm. 'When you gave him his freedom, you promised *never* to rub that lamp again!'

'Who is Abdul?' inquired the Son and Heir.

'He's the Slave of the Lamp,' said the Emperor Aladdin. 'But you wouldn't know about the Lamp. When I was but a boy, my Wicked Uncle Abanazar sent me down into a cave to find it, and then he sealed me up there. In my alarm, I chanced to rub the Lamp by Accident, and Abdul appeared and told me I had but to Command and he would Obey. Well, to cut a long story short, I took him at his word and that, my child, was how I met your mother. While it's perfectly true that I promised him I wouldn't bother him again, I'm *sure* he'll realize that I have no other choice, faced with an emergency such as this!'

He clapped his hands for a Lady-in-Waiting who had been conveniently listening outside the door.

'Kindly bring the Lamp,' he ordered rather grandly, being nervous, 'and try not to rub it against anything on the way.'

'I'll be *sure* not to!' said the Lady-in-Waiting with heartfelt sincerity.

[6]

'Of course, it may not even work any more,' he said as the Lady-in-Waiting departed, wearing her uneasiest expression, 'but if *anyone*'ll know what to do, Abdul will!'

'Never say I didn't warn you!' said the Widow Twankey, more grimly than before. 'If he takes it the wrong way and creates an Ugly Scene, I shall *not* be party to it!'

The Lady-in-Waiting came back with the Lamp at arm's length, and as soon as the Emperor Aladdin took it, she disappeared so fast it hardly seemed possible.

The Emperor Aladdin held up the Lamp cautiously between his finger and thumb.

'Well, well, well,' he said slowly, looking at it from one end and then from the other and, finally, sideways. 'And to think I once handled it as casually as tap your top-knot! Well, here we go; ready or not!'

'I *still* say he won't come; but if he does, tell me after he's gone! I'm not going to look!' announced the Widow Twankey, putting her fingers in her ears and screwing her eyes tight shut.

She looked so absurd that the Son and Heir was unable to repress a giggle.

The Emperor Aladdin glanced over at him in reproach.

'I don't think *you* ought to look either,' he advised him gravely. 'Abdul's hardly what you'd call handsome!'

'Why, the uglier the better!' his Son and Heir assured him cheerfully, leaning over the end of his cot. 'So rub the Lamp, Papa, unless you're too scared!'

The Emperor Aladdin stiffened, and the Widow Twankey opened one eye.

'Haven't you rubbed it *yet*?' she demanded indignantly.

For answer, a loud clap of thunder resounded through the room.

The Widow Twankey flung the Lamp in the air, dug her fingers back into her ears, and squeezed her eyes twice as tightly shut as before.

The Emperor Aladdin and his Son and Heir were too

preoccupied to notice. They were watching the floor, which was slowly cracking open down the middle.

As the thunder died away, a large cloud of green smoke rose up through the crack in the floor, and hovered imposingly in the middle of the room.

Then the floor closed, leaving no sign of the crack, and slowly and impressively Abdul's huge green saucer-eyes began to glow like lamps.

His big bulbous nose appeared next, with a bright brass ring in it, and then his big wide mouth, with long white walrus tusks at either end. Next came his carefully combed whiskers, then his glittering jade-green earrings, and his tall turreted turquoise turban; after that the last of the green smoke cleared away, and he slowly came to rest on the floor.

'I am the Slave of the Lamp! Ask what you wilt, and it shall be done!' he boomed in a voice like a hollow gong falling down an empty well. 'And this is a fine time to ask it!' he added plaintively. 'I was in my bath!'

'Oh, dear! How inconvenient! But it's delightful to see

you again, my dear Abdul!' said the Emperor Aladdin ingratiatingly.

'What is your wish, Master?' said the Djinn, unbending only slightly.

'I'm in urgent need of your good advice,' said the Emperor Aladdin. 'Won't you sit down?'

Abdul shook his head.

'Don't you remember? I burn through chairs,' he said. 'Advice of what nature?'

'The problem concerns my Son and Heir,' continued the Emperor Aladdin, pointing to the cot.

'Oho, so you're a father now?' said Abdul, studying the Son and Heir judiciously. 'My congratulations on a fine, normal, healthy boy! How can *he* present a problem?'

'I talk,' the Son and Heir said pleasantly.

Abdul's eyebrows shot up under his turban.

'He speaks quite fluently,' the Emperor Aladdin explained apologetically. 'I was just about to tell you. That's why I rubbed the Lamp. To ask you what to do!'

'The Widow Twankey swears it's a Spell,' the Son and Heir put in helpfully, 'but we think not.'

'It's certainly not an ordinary, common-or-garden Spell,' the Djinn agreed slowly. 'I don't remember having come across a case like this before . . . I have a son myself, in a quiet sort of way, but all *he* says is *Boomalakka Wee*.'

'Just *Boomalakka Wee*?' asked the Emperor Aladdin.

'Just *Boomalakka Wee*.'

'Not another word?'

'Not another word.'

The Emperor Aladdin permitted himself a sigh.

'You must be very proud of having a son who can only say *Boomalakka Wee*,' he said in a slightly envious voice.

The Djinn realized he had not been tactful.

'Well, yes; but then again, it *can* get monotonous,' he confessed. 'Though I'm not sure I'd want it any different; at least not until he's teethed. But about *your* boy, now. I'm just trying to remember something,' he added, screwing up one eye and tugging a whisker to help him concentrate. 'It's on the fork of my tongue! I must walk up and down!'

He walked up and down, burning four holes in a valuable carpet that lay in his path.

'*Ginger!*' he exclaimed imposingly, halting in front of Aladdin. 'Does that convey anything?'

'An edible seasoning?' suggested the Emperor Aladdin hopefully.

'I have it!' cried the Djinn, slapping his forehead so hard that green sparks flew in the air. 'The Land of Green Ginger! It all comes back to me now! The Land of Green Ginger,' announced the Djinn impressively, 'was built by a Magician who was very fond of fresh vegetables. The idea was that when he went travelling, he could take the Land of Green Ginger with him like a portable kitchen-garden; only fancier, if you follow me? But something went wrong with the final spell. *You* know how it is; there's always an element of risk. Well, this final spell went wrong, and turned him into a Button-Nosed Tortoise; and the poor man has never been able to turn himself back!'

'Imagine that!' cried the Son and Heir.

'Proceed!' begged the Emperor, all ears.

'The *rest* of the spells worked perfectly, however,' Abdul proceeded, 'so while the Magician was busy trying to turn himself back into a Magician – which was, naturally, his immediate concern – the Land of Green Ginger suddenly floated off on its own, away into nowhere!'

'Why didn't the Magician make it fly back down again?' the Son and Heir inquired rather sensibly.

'If *you* were a Button-Nosed Tortoise, would *you* be able to control a complicated thing like a flying kitchen-garden?' asked the Djinn. 'Indeed you would *not*! And as nobody *else* knows how to control it, it just floats wherever its fancy takes it. It's always where you'd *least* expect it to be. For example, a tired traveller might go to sleep on a barren desert, and wake up with his feet up a tree and his head on a mushroom. That would give *anyone* cause for confusion, would it not?'

'It would indeed!' agreed the Emperor Aladdin. 'But how does all this concern my Son and Heir?'

'What were the first words he uttered?' requested the Djinn. 'Don't tell me – I *know*! He said "Button-Nosed Tortoise"! Am I right? I see by your face I'm right! Your son,' proclaimed the Djinn impressively, 'is the one chosen to break the spell of the Land of Green Ginger, and restore the Magician to his normal shape! It's all been foretold, you see – nothing has been left to chance. I can even tell you your son's name. It's Abu Ali!'

'Abu Ali?' repeated the Emperor Aladdin experimentally. 'I like it *much* better than Tea Pot or Bird's Nest Soup!'

'Now tell me how I break the spell, and when?' asked Abu Ali, quite willing to set about it there and then.

'As soon as you come of age,' said Abdul.

At this point, the Widow Twankey's loud voice reminded them of her presence, in spite of the fact that she still kept her fingers in her ears and her eyes tight shut.

'Aladdin!' she called. 'Has the obnoxious creature gone yet?'

'Long ago, Mamma,' said the Emperor Aladdin diplomatically. 'The only person with us now is Dear Old Abdul.'

Abdul concentrated his glittering gaze on the Widow Twankey's portly contours.

'You know, your mother always *was* a little too verbal,' he said thoughtfully. 'Wouldn't she be more valuable to collectors if she were to stay like that?'

'Now, now, Abdul!' began the Emperor Aladdin nervously.

'However, my time is up, Master. Calm your fears. All is as it should be. Peace be with you! Going *Down*!'

He stamped his foot. Instantly there was another loud rumble of thunder, the floor obligingly split open, and Abdul sank down into it. Less than a moment later, there was nothing to show that he had ever been there, save for a faint swirl of green smoke which hovered in the air for a moment, and then wafted out the window.

'Well, *now* we know the answer to the problem, so we can all relax!' said little Abu Ali with satisfaction, sitting back in his cot.

The Emperor Aladdin turned to the Widow Twankey.

'Abdul's gone, Mamma!' he said cheerfully. 'You can open your eyes now!'

But the Widow Twankey continued to keep her eyes tight shut and her fingers in her ears.

'Mamma!' called the Emperor Aladdin in a louder voice, tapping her with his fan. 'He's gone!'

They waited. But the Widow Twankey never so much as twitched.

'Give her a push, Papa,' suggested Abu Ali helpfully. 'Just a *small* one, to begin with.'

The Emperor Aladdin gave the Widow Twankey a *small* push; and all she did was rock gently to and fro, and then come to rest again in exactly the same position.

Little Abu Ali's face broke into a beaming smile.

'*Kind* Old Abdul!' he said happily. 'He's arranged it so she'll stay like that!'

Yes indeed, gentle reader, Abdul had done exactly that!

What more impressive way to end a chapter?

Chapter The Second

*Which Explains How Abu Ali Began the Search for
the Land of Green Ginger, and Introduces Us to
the Wicked Prince Tintac Ping Foo*

In due course Prince Abu Ali came of age, and the Grand
Vizier, who was now well advanced in age and had to wear
quartz spectacles, called a special meeting of state in the
White Lacquer Room of the Palace.

The White Lacquer Room was now enhanced by a
handsome decorative ornament, which stood on a marble
pedestal at the far end.

Yes, gentle reader, you have guessed correctly.

It was the Widow Twankey, who *still* had her fingers in
her ears and her eyes tight shut; and she was dusted daily,
in the morning; for no matter how often the Emperor
Aladdin rubbed the Lamp, Abdul had never once appeared
again.

The special meeting arrived promptly, as was its wont,
and seated itself in a circle on the white silk mats, with one
notable absentee. The Master of the Horse had been
requested not to invite his friend.

Upon the arrival of the Emperor Aladdin, the Empress
Bedr-el-Budur, and the Prince Abu Ali, everyone present
stood up and bowed while the Royal Family seated itself on
three special thrones.

And, even though he *is* the hero of this tale, Prince Abu
Ali had his faults, gentle reader, and it is now my painful
duty to enumerate them.

He was too amiable; too good-natured; too kindly; too
honest, and too fair-minded.

He was far too considerate of other people's feelings.

He laughed too easily, and he was much too sympathetic.

He was deeply fond of both his parents.

He was never lazy, impudent, or ill-mannered.

He could never raise his voice in foolish rage, or be a tattle-tale behind your back.

He was, in fact, *quite* hopeless. Nobody in the Court could see any hope for him. They were sure he'd make a highly unsuccessful Emperor. They doubted whether he would even be able to make a good marriage; because any *real* Princess was bound to find him as dull as ditchwater.

The problem presented by these serious flaws was uppermost in the minds of the special meeting when the Grand Vizier beat on the Dragon Gong with his Ivory Wand.

'Your Imperial Majesties!' he began ceremoniously. 'Also, Your Imperial Highness! Also, Lords and Ladies of the Court! We are met here (with the exception of the friend of the Master of the Horse, who has been sent to his room till teatime), to give formal voice to our unworthy joy at the very important event of the coming of age of the Heir Apparent, Prince Abu Ali!'

Here he bowed low to Prince Abu Ali, and everyone present applauded.

Prince Abu Ali rose and graciously returned the bow.

It was a charming ritual, marred only by the Grand Vizier's inability to straighten up after *his* bow.

When he had been tactfully restored to his normal height by the Master of the Horse (who never bore malice), he tapped the Dragon Gong again, and everyone present stopped applauding.

'We are gathered here,' he proceeded, 'to decide what female of suitably affluent status shall be given the honour of Prince Abu Ali's hand in marriage!'

'Can't hear! What did he say?' muttered the Lord Chamberlain testily.

'You have *each* been given', said the Grand Vizier, pretending not to have heard the Lord Chamberlain, 'a piece of paper –'

'*I* haven't!' objected the Lord Chamberlain at once. '*Nor* a pencil! I suppose you thought I wouldn't notice? Well, I *did*!'

This threw the Grand Vizier into such a tizzwoz that he dropped his notes all over the floor.

While the Master of the Horse was selflessly retrieving them, Prince Abu Ali took command of the floor.

'Forgive me, one and all,' he said courteously but firmly. 'But before we proceed further, I wish to make my position quite clear, to avoid confusion later.'

'*Thank* you!' said the Grand Vizier, mistaking this for a vote of confidence.

'The actual choice of my bride elect must, of course, be entirely my own,' proceeded Prince Abu Ali.

'No pencil!' whined the Lord Chamberlain.

'But that's unconstitutional!' cried the Grand Vizier, deeply shocked.

'Well, it will have to be constitutional *this* time,' said Abu Ali pleasantly, 'or there'll *be* no bride-elect!'

'He's a dear, headstrong boy!' cooed the Empress Bedr-el-Budur dotingly.

'Are we agreed, then?' asked Abu Ali politely.

'*No!*' said the Grand Vizier.

'Yes!' piped the Lord Chamberlain, and everyone present applauded. Hoping to do so unobserved, the Grand Vizier hit the Lord Chamberlain with his fan, and the Lord Chamberlain hit him right back, knocking off his quartz glasses.

It was a most regrettable incident, only saved from further deterioration by the Master of the Horse, who discreetly confiscated both their fans.

'Let us proceed, then, to the matter of the Land of Green Ginger,' said Abu Ali, decorum having been restored. 'On the day of my birth, the Slave of the Lamp told me that I was the person chosen to break the spell; but he departed without telling me *how*. Well, no pains have been spared to re-establish communication with Abdul, but none has had the desired effect. I suggest that the reason for this is that Abdul thinks we still want him to restore the Queen Mother to her former state; and we can all understand his disinclination to improve on nature.'

Everybody present nodded wisely, and then quickly shook their heads.

'I therefore suggest that if we promise never to mention the subject of the Queen Mother, Abdul will appear when we rub the Lamp. Which I have with me,' he added, holding up the Lamp, 'because I am so confident of your magnanimous cooperation.'

Everybody present was so profoundly gratified that they all nodded; except the Grand Vizier, who had sunk into an *appalling* sulk.

'Have I your approval, Father?' asked Abu Ali. 'May I summon Abdul?'

The Emperor Aladdin, though indulgent to a fault, hesitated.

'Yes, dear. Of course he may!' prompted the Empress Bedr-el-Budur dotingly.

'Thank you!' said Abu Ali, and rubbed his sleeve across the Lamp. 'Abdul; if you obey this summons, nobody will mention the little matter of the Widow Twankey!'

There was an expectant hush that grew longer and longer; but just as everybody present was beginning to feel happier about the whole thing, a sudden rumble of thunder shook the Palace, the floor cracked open, and the huge cloud of green smoke rose impressively and hovered in the air.

'I am the Slave of the Lamp! Ask what thou wilt and it shall be done!' boomed Abdul's voice, as he slowly came to rest on the floor.

'*Oooh-ahh!*' shrilled the Lord Chamberlain, realizing at last what was afoot; and, very sensibly for a man of his advanced years, fainted away.

'I notice you answer promptly enough when my *son* rubs the Lamp!' said the Emperor Aladdin to Abdul in modulated reproach.

'I don't *have* to answer the Lamp for *anyone*! I only did it for him as a favour!' the Djinn replied tartly.

'Exactly!' agreed Abu Ali smoothly. 'And I know that I speak for everyone present, when I tell you how uncommonly grateful we are!'

'Thank you, young man!' said the Genie, palpably flattered. 'So you've come of age, at last! Well, what can I do for you, other than wish you a Happy Birthday? If it's the whereabouts of the Land of Green Ginger, you've come to the wrong Djinn. You have to find it yourself!'

'I'm quite ready and willing to do that!' Abu Ali assured him respectfully. 'But I *would* be grateful for a tip or two!'

'I like your manners. You're a polite young man,' said Abdul approvingly. 'But we Djinns have to watch out for spells that have gone wrong! I'll tell *this* much, though. You'll run afoul of the wicked Prince Tintac Ping Foo of Persia, and the wicked Prince Rubdub Ben Thud of Arabia. Don't trust either of them farther than you could push a peck of peppercorns up a perpendicular precipice!'

'I'll remember that!' vowed Abu Ali.

'And,' Abdul continued, '*if* you do get into serious trouble – and one invariably does – I'll allow you *one* rub of the Lamp. *Only one, mind!* And before you rub it, be sure your need is urgent! Don't waste it on something trivial, like a drink of water because you feel hot . . . you wouldn't believe it, but I've known many a ninny do just that! He only does it once, though! He gets the drink of water all right; but it drops out of a clear sky on to his head, and it's in a jug!'

'I'll remember that too!' Abu Ali assured him devoutly.

'And while I think of it,' added Abdul, a little *too* casually, '*if* you just so *happen* to call in at Samarkand, you might do worse than inquire after the health of Silver Bud, the only daughter of Sulkpot Ben Nagnag the Jeweller.'

'Why? Is she my destined Bride-to-Be?' asked Abu Ali alertly.

'I don't say Yes, and I don't say No,' said Abdul pro-vocatively. 'I only say that *if* you *do* inquire after her health, who knows what it may lead to? By the way,' he added insincerely, 'I've forgotten the spell that restores decorative ornaments to humdrum life. Does anybody mind?'

[18]

'Not in the *slightest*!' said the Empress Bedr-el-Budur, smiling dotingly at Abu Ali.

'I'll say farewell, then!' said Abdul. 'Going *Down*!'

He stamped his foot; the floor split open; he vanished feet first, turban last; and the usual wisp of green smoke drifted out of the window.

Everybody present drew a deep breath of relief and began feeling themselves tenderly all over to make sure they hadn't been turned into additional decorative ornaments.

Now by a curious coincidence, gentle reader, it so happened that on the identical day that Abu Ali set out from Peking in China to seek the Land of Green Ginger, the Shah of Persia sent a politely worded invitation to his son, the vapid, vindictive Prince Tintac Ping Foo; requesting the dubious honour of his presence on a matter of urgent importance; and after Prince Tintac Ping Foo had deliberately kept the Shah of Persia waiting for forty-two minutes, he haughtily presented himself.

'Ah, Tintac Ping Foo,' said the Shah of Persia ingratiatingly, 'I want to have a friendly, man-to-man, equal-to-equal, father-to-son talk with you, my boy.'

'Oh, you do, do you?' riposted Tintac Ping Foo ungraciously. 'Well, if it's about cheating at chess, I wouldn't bother, because I *adore* cheating at chess; I shall continue to cheat at chess; and if you *dare* to stop me, I shall put glue in your beard!'

'Now, now, now,' said the Shah of Persia soothingly. 'It's not about chess. Cheat as much as you want to. But forget about that glue, there's a good lad,' he added uneasily. 'A joke at the expense of your elders is a joke, and I can enjoy it with the next man; but glue in a beard is glue in a beard!'

'What, then, is the purpose of this tedious confabulation?' demanded Tintac Ping Foo, making no promises about the glue.

'My son,' began the Shah. 'Don't you think it is time you wed?'

'Say that again and I'll stamp on your great big gouty foot!' his foppish offspring warned him, his nostrils pinched and pink. 'Why, in all the world, there's *no one* good enough for *me!*'

'Agreed, agreed!' the Shah of Persia pacified him. 'But unless you settle for the best there is, my son, our illustrious line will expire; and we don't want that, now, do we? Have you ever heard of Silver Bud of Samarkand?'

'No, and I don't want to!' snapped his snooty offspring.

'Even though she is beautiful beyond all dreams?' asked the Shah temptingly. 'And her father Sulkpot Ben Nagnag is the richest wholesale jeweller in all Araby?'

'How rich is that?' asked the Wicked Prince Tintac Ping Foo in a much more interested voice. 'Let me have the exact figures, and I *might* think about it – though I promise nothing, mind you!' he added quickly.

'The exact figures can be obtained from the Court Treasurer,' said the Shah of Persia. 'I would gladly leave you to browse through them at your leisure, except that my spies (who are everywhere) have secretly informed me that a rival suitor for the lady's hand has lately come upon the scene.'

'Name names!' demanded the Wicked Prince Tintac Ping Foo, scowling in a truly horrid manner.

'Prince Rubdub Ben Thud of Arabia.'

'*What?* Rubdub Ben *Thud*?' shrilled the Wicked Prince in fiercest ire. 'That balloon-faced butterball? Do you *dare* to tell me he has the silly sauce to pit himself against a paragon of lovable manly virtues like me?'

'I'm afraid so. Yes,' said the Shah of Persia gravely.

'Oh, har! Oh, har! Oh, *har*!' scoffed Tintac Ping Foo scornfully. 'I'd like to be there when they throw him out on his ear; but it's *far* too far beneath my delicate dignity!'

'I quite agree,' agreed his father insincerely, 'and I'd laugh as loudly as you, my son; except that my spies inform me that Sulkpot Ben Nagnag looks with favour on his suit, and has invited him to lunch.'

The Wicked Prince Tintac Ping Foo went as purple in the face as a stick of jealous rhubarb, and shook his fists towards the sky.

'Then woe betide Rubdub Ben Thud!' he vowed vindictively. 'He'll rue the day he crossed my path! Ho there, Slaves! My camels! My retinue! My magic sword! My jellybeans! I leave at once for Samarkand!'

And what is more, gentle reader, he meant it, and he *did*.

Chapter The Third

Which Explains How Abu Ali Met the Wicked Princes
Tintac Ping Foo and Rubdub Ben Thud for the First Time

The footlingly fatuous, awesomely overweight Prince Rubdub Ben Thud lay back in a reinforced heliotrope hammock, singing to himself. The hammock hung between the two strongest palm trees in the Last Oasis But One before Samarkand, and the Wicked Prince Rubdub Ben Thud's retinue had camped there for the night.

He was singing a song he had composed entirely without professional assistance. It went:

Kadoo, kadunk, kadee,

Kadee, kadunk, kadoo,
Kadunk,
Kadoole – Ooodle – Dunk!

He was accompanied on the tom-tom by his diabolically devious devotee, Small Slave, who sat near enough to the hammock to enable him to swing it gently with one toe.

'What is your *absolutely* honest opinion of that last verse?' asked the Wicked Prince Rubdub Ben Thud, suddenly breaking off in mid-trill and eyeing Small Slave searchingly.

'It was as the coo of nightingales, only more exquisite, O Prince of Song,' answered Small Slave absolutely honestly. 'Pray continue these melodious murmurs from your luscious larynx, or I shall expire before your very eyes.'

'You were a little late on the tom-tom with that last *Kadunk*,' his Master answered, pleased but just a mite severe.

'Only my fatuous stupidity prevented me from anticipating it, O Prince of the Golden Voice heard only in ecstatic dreams!' Small Slave assured him humbly.

'Then we'll try it again – and this time be more careful. Ready? *Kadoo, Kadunk, Ka*wait a moment!' grunted the Wicked Prince Rubdub Ben Thud. 'I can hear camel bells! Can you?'

Small Slave listened carefully.

'Many,' he confirmed. 'Distinctly.'

'Coming here!' added the Wicked Prince Rubdub Ben Thud indignantly. 'Reely; there's no privacy *anywhere*! This is *my* Oasis! I got here first! Go and tell them to be off!'

'Instantly, O Prince of Song,' said Small Slave, trying to unhitch his toe from the hammock rope; by which time the alien Caravan was upon them, and seated on the front camel was none other than the Wicked Prince Tintac Ping Foo in pompous person.

The sight was so unwelcome that the Wicked Prince

Rubdub Ben Thud rolled out of the hammock and on to his feet without even realizing he had done it.

'Ping Foo!' he hissed beneath his breath, grinding many of his teeth in rabid rage. 'Can it be possible that he is my rival for the hand of Silver Bud?'

The Wicked Prince Tintac Ping Foo, having halted his camel, dismounted effortlessly by falling on his head.

When his retinue had picked him up, both Princes bowed ceremoniously to each other.

'Allah be with you and protect you, most noble and illustrious Rubdub Ben Thud!' said Ping Foo hypocritically.

'Allah be with you and protect *you*, most illustrious and noble Tintac Ping Foo!' returned Rubdub just as hypocritically, if not more so.

'You're not going to Samarkand by whilom chance?' asked Tintac Ping Foo.

Rubdub gave an airy laugh.

'Bless me, no!' he said. '*You're* not going there by whilom chance, are you?'

Tintac Ping Foo gave an even airier laugh.

'Whatever made you think *that*?' he inquired jocosely. '*I'm* off to Yokohama to hunt yak!'

'Indeed, indeed?' said Rubdub Ben Thud with a laugh that was not so much airy as downright draughty. 'You won't be staying the night here, then?'

'How amusing that you should ask me that!' riposted the Wicked Prince Tintac Ping Foo gaily.

'Ooo, I wouldn't if *I* were you!' Rubdub Ben Thud warned him solicitously. 'The sand here is *terribly* sandy, and the water tastes *awful*! I shouldn't be surprised if there aren't a lot of mosquitoes about, too!'

'I shouldn't either,' agreed Tintac Ping Foo blandly.

'Then you *surely* won't stay?' Rubdub Ben Thud urged him anxiously.

'Ah, yes. Ah, yes, I will, Rubdub Ben Thud,' returned Tintac Ping Foo sweetly, 'for the simple reason that we're both going to Samarkand, and well we both know it!'

'I must ask you to explain that remark!' demanded Rubdub, bristling.

'Willingly!' giggled Ping Foo. 'When Silver Bud sees *you*, she'll faint with laughter!'

'Oh, she will, will she?' growled Rubdub grimly. 'Well, when she sees *you*, she'll die of fright!'

The Wicked Prince Tintac Ping Foo cut short his giggle.

'Fatty!' he said insultingly.

'Clothes-horse! Bean-pole! Fop!' snarled Rubdub.

'Sausage! Football! Tub!' jeered Tintac.

And it was at this crucial moment, gentle reader, that Abu Ali came riding into the Oasis on his White Charger.

Both Wicked Princes surveyed him with immediate suspicion.

Abu Ali, well aware of their hostility, watched his manners and bowed courteously.

'Good evening,' he said in a friendly voice.

'Who might *you* be?' replied the Wicked Prince Tintac Ping Foo, refusing to bow back.

[25]

'Abu Ali,' said Abu Ali. 'Who might *you* be?'

'I could *only* be Prince Tintac Ping Foo of Persia!' answered Ping Foo rudely. 'And that turnip in tantrums can only be Prince Rubdub Ben Thud of Arabia!'

'Your obedient servant, gentlemen,' said Abu Ali, still civil.

Rubdub pulled a face and turned his back.

'Where are you going?' proceeded Ping Foo. 'Not to Samarkand, by any chance?'

'No, indeed,' said Abu Ali wisely. 'I'm looking for the Land of Green Ginger.'

'Never heard of it!' said Ping Foo disrespectfully.

'Me neither!' added Rubdub, all ears.

'Fortunately I have,' said Abu Ali politely, 'so I'll stay the night here, and press on tomorrow,' whereupon he began to unsaddle his White Charger.

As the Wicked Princes had suspected at one and the same moment that Abu Ali could *only* be a third rival for the hand of Silver Bud, they now began to tiptoe stealthily towards one another.

'He's a rival, Rubdub!' hissed the Wicked Prince Tintac Ping Foo in a hostile hiss. 'We must plot and plan!'

'Very well,' conceded Rubdub. 'You plot, and I'll plan, and then we'll add it up and divide by two!'

'We must poison him!' Prince Tintac Ping Foo decided, after a long plot. 'Have you any?'

'I'm very much afraid, none,' answered Rubdub regretfully. 'Suppose we boil him in oil instead?'

'What oil?' countered Tintac Ping Foo.

'Small Slave might know of some,' said Rubdub hopefully. 'Small Slave, do you know of any oil?'

'We have a little,' said Small Slave. 'Just enough for breakfast.'

'Ah, well, we won't touch *that*,' said Rubdub hastily. 'Why not shoot him with your bow-and-arrow, Foo?'

'Because I often miss!' replied Tintac Ping Foo irritably.

'Then creep up behind him and push him into the pool,

then keep your foot on his head till the bubbles come up!'
suggested Rubdub brightly.

'I like the idea,' conceded Tintac Ping Foo moodily.
'Except for the fact that *he* might push first!'

'Oh, come. You have to take the rough with the smooth,'
said Rubdub.

'Fools rush in where wise men fear to tread!' Ping Foo
reminded him.

'A stitch in time saves nine!' countered Rubdub.

'Least said, soonest mended!' parried Ping Foo.

'If your illustrious highnesses will permit an untouchable
to make a worthless suggestion,' Small Slave broke in, 'why
not make friends with the fellow?'

'You're mad!' gasped Ping Foo.

'Bubble-brained!' snorted Rubdub.

'Then you can invite him to supper, and drug his wine.
After which you can steal his White Charger and depart for
Samarkand without him harming a hair of your heads!'
said Small Slave patiently.

'*Is* that the best solution?' asked Rubdub uncertainly,
after a pause.

'Indisputably,' Small Slave assured him.

'Then I'm glad I thought of it first!' said Rubdub
unselfishly.

'I beg your pardon! *I* thought of it first, so *I'll* do the
inviting!' Ping Foo corrected him, nipping all further argu-
ment in the bud by strolling over to Abu Ali.

'Ah, there, Abu Ali!' he said in a voice of rancid roguery.
'Would you care to take supper with us? Just pot-luck, so to
speak; but you'd be very welcome!'

'How very kind! I'd be delighted!' said Abu Ali.

'Splendid!' said the Wicked Prince Tintac Ping Foo. 'We'll
expect you, then!'

He hurried back to the Wicked Prince Rubdub Ben Thud,
and began to plan the supper at once, dish by dish. The
Wicked Prince Rubdub Ben Thud ordered double helpings

of everything, which was only to be expected, and finally Small Slave mixed a powerful poison into a jug of their best wine. The jug had a dab of red sealing wax on it to warn the Princes never to drink from it *on any account*.

The supper went off well (though Abu Ali never ate anything till the Wicked Princes had helped themselves first); and all might have gone as Small Slave had intended, if the Wicked Prince Tintac Ping Foo hadn't felt called upon to show off. He *insisted* on doing two rather feeble tricks with a polkadot bandana.

'Well, upon my *word*!' said Rubdub, who was easily taken in by tricks, even the feeblest. 'Amazing! Do some more!'

'Nothing would delight me more,' Ping Foo assured him smugly. 'But for my best trick, I need a Gold Coin. If you care to lend me one, I guarantee to amaze you!'

The *last* thing the Wicked Prince Rubdub Ben Thud wanted to do was lend the Wicked Prince Tintac Ping Foo money; but his curiosity had got the better of him. He handed Tintac Ping Foo a shiny new gold coin *just* as Small Slave was setting the special jug of poisoned wine in front of Abu Ali.

'The wine, Your Highness!' said Small Slave significantly; but Rubdub waved him to silence, his eye glued to his gold coin.

'Keep your eye on this coin!' admonished Ping Foo, taking it and biting it carefully. 'Now watch me closely! I wrap the hanky around it – *so* – and wave my fingers over it – *so* – and the gold coin has now turned into a small brown pebble!'

There was an eloquent silence for a full minute.

'A small brown pebble?' inquired the Wicked Prince Rubdub Ben Thud in a strangled contralto.

'A small brown pebble,' nodded Ping Foo, holding it out for him to see.

There was no mistake. It was a small brown pebble.

Rubdub gazed at it till his eyes began to water, and

finally he was able to say, my, how clever it all was; and would Tintac Ping Foo kindly turn the small brown pebble back into his gold coin at *once*, please?

'Ah, that's *quite* another kettle of fish, I'm afraid!' said Tintac Ping Foo with polite regret. 'But you may keep the small brown pebble.'

'I don't want the small brown pebble!' rasped Ben Thud hoarsely. 'I want my gold coin!'

'But the small brown pebble *is* your gold coin,' Ping Foo explained patiently.

'You mean you *can't* change it back?' quavered Rubdub, while spots began to dance before his eyes.

'I'm afraid not.'

'By all that peals and thunders!' squeaked Rubdub fiercely. 'I've been robbed! Give me back my gold coin before I punch you in one of your tiny pink eyes; you long-nosed, nobbly-kneed nincompoop!'

'Long-nosed? Nobbly-kneed?' echoed the incensed Ping Foo. 'You just wait till Silver Bud has to choose between us!'

'Jealousy!' bellowed Rubdub, flinging caution to the winds. 'Jealousy of a better man!'

'What utter piffle!' shrilled Tintac Ping Foo. 'You're not a man! You're a football!'

'*Withdraw that!*' screamed Rubdub fiercely.

'*Football! Football! Football!* There! Now challenge me to mortal combat!' Ping Foo dared him fecklessly. 'Go on! I double dare you!'

'Very well, I *will*!' roared Rubdub. 'I challenge you to mortal combat! There! Sucks boo!'

'Gentlemen, this is *so* rash!' Small Slave warned them glumly. 'I *do* advise you to –'

'You fetch my sword, and keep your advice to yourself!' smouldered Rubdub darkly. 'The Magic Sword I killed that Dragon with, remember? And hurry up! I killed a Dragon with that Sword!' he added impressively to Ping Foo. 'I bought it from a genuine dervish!'

'I bought mine from a genuine dervish, too, and it *also* kills dragons!' boasted Ping Foo, drawing his sword and waving it in the air.

'Oh,' said Rubdub, cooling down a little. 'I wonder if it could have been the same genuine dervish?'

Ping Foo stopped waving his sword.

'Which kind of genuine dervish did you buy yours from?' he asked, doubt creeping into his voice.

'A whirling one, in Timbuktoo,' said Rubdub.

'The one with the small shop in the High Street?' asked Ping Foo, more doubtful than before.

'Yes,' said Rubdub, now quite cooled down.

'Was his name Ghoulghoul ben Guava?'

'Yes, it was.'

'He told me my sword was the only one like it in the world,' said Ping Foo deflatedly.

'That's what he told *me*,' said Rubdub.

At this moment, Small Slave brought him his Magic Sword. Rubdub held it beside Ping Foo's.

'Exactly the same!' he said emotionally.

'But *exactly*!' agreed Ping Foo. 'I'd like a word with that dervish! I paid twenty gold pieces for this sword!'

'Twenty?' cried Rubdub. 'Lumbering lobster pots! He charged me thirty! If ever I see that dervish again, I'll boil him in oil!'

'If I may be allowed a word in edgeways,' said Small Slave practically, 'your immediate enemy is Abu Ali; and *he* rode off to Samarkand as soon as you spilt the beans!'

'HE DID WHAT?' cried the Wicked Prince Tintac Ping Foo, slapping at a palm tree in his petulant pique.

'See for yourselves!' said Small Slave, pointing.

Far away in the distance, they saw a small speck dwindling to an ever smaller one in the moonlight.

'Foiled!' blubbered Rubdub. 'Foiled, by all that peals and thunders!' and he was shaken with such emotion that he fell flat on his back, and it took the combined efforts of everybody present to get him back on to his feet; for the Wicked Prince Rubdub Ben Thud was taller, lying down, than he was standing up. He never would have been able to get up unaided, not if he had tried all night.

Chapter The Fourth

Which Explains How Abu Ali Met a Friend

Abu Ali reached Samarkand so early the next morning that no one was awake.

As he climbed off his White Charger in the empty Market Place, however, he heard an unusually cheerful voice singing in the next street.

When it suddenly broke off, Abu Ali hurried around the corner and found out why. The singer had tripped carelessly off the sidewalk and was now lying flat on his back in the middle of the road.

Abu Ali helped him up, though the singer did very little to assist, being quite helpless with laughter.

'I hope you came to no harm?' asked Abu Ali pleasantly.

'None whatever!' the singer assured him merrily. 'But

thank you for asking; and a *good*, good morning! Would you care to buy a tent?'

'Some other time, perhaps,' said Abu Ali. 'Are you trying to sell one?'

'*One?*' exclaimed the singer. 'One? I sell *thousands*! I *make* them! Khayyam's the name – Omar Khayyam! My shop's just down the street – anything from pup tents for picnics, on up! You *did* say you'd breakfast with me? Very nice horse, that. I had a horse once. They go for days without water, don't they? No, no – that's camels! By the way, don't take it amiss, but I've forgotten your name.'

'Abu Ali,' said Abu Ali. 'And about that breakfast –'

'I wouldn't hear of it, my dear fellow! *You* shall have it with *me*! No, no, I *insist*! One moment, while I find my shop –'

He looked carefully up and down the street.

'– *try* and find my shop!' he corrected himself. 'It appears to have been done away with!'

Abu Ali looked up and down the street too, and then saw a sign directly over their heads which read:

OMAR KHAYYAM

TENTMAKER

NO CONNECTION WITH ANY OTHER FIRM

'I think we're here,' he suggested.

'Are we? Well, I never! So we are!' said Omar Khayyam, pleasantly surprised. 'Now where's my key? Did I forget to take it with me? Yes, I did! How provoking; now we'll *never* get into the shop!' he said, opening the door. 'And mind the step,' he added, falling down it immediately. 'Funny how *everyone* does that,' he added as Abu Ali helped him up again. 'But business is bad everywhere. Now, *you* wait here, and I'll see what there is in the pantry!'

Abu Ali felt that Omar Khayyam, though a little absent-minded, was someone who could be trusted as a friend in need; nor was he proved wrong. After breakfast Omar Khayyam listened to his story with sympathetic attention, and only shook his head when Abu Ali explained that he must find Silver Bud as soon as possible, if not sooner.

'Alas, my friend,' he told him sadly, 'it is clear you know very little about that rapacious rapscallion, Sulkpot Ben Nagnag!'

'I know little or nothing about him,' admitted Abu Ali. 'Will he present obstacles?'

'A thousand!' said Omar Khayyam glumly. 'He locks up poor Silver Bud like a prisoner!'

'What? His own daughter? For what reason?' exclaimed Abu Ali, unable to believe his ears.

'The reason is all too plain!' answered Omar Khayyam sadly. 'The old rogue is terrified she'll fall in love with some upright lad of no account, like you or sometimes even me. Whereas he intends to marry her to a *Prince*!'

'Any kind of Prince?' asked Abu Ali attentively.

'Oh, *no*!' said Omar Khayyam. 'He'd have to be *rich* and royal, and the *direct* heir to whatever throne he's Prince of!'

'Then I have nothing to fear! I'm the sole heir to the Throne of China!' said Abu Ali simply.

Omar Khayyam shook his amiable head.

'I'm sorry, but you wouldn't fool him, not for a *moment*,' he answered kindly.

'But I *am* the Prince of China!' insisted Abu Ali, somewhat taken aback.

Omar Khayyam shook his amiable head again.

'I like you, and I like your horse, but I don't believe you're a Prince, and you couldn't make me,' he declared regretfully. 'Are you cross?'

'Not at all,' said Abu Ali peaceably. 'You've done me a very good turn. Now I know better than to tell people I'm a Prince! But no matter *who* you think I am, can I leave an innocent maid to the mercies of Rubdub Ben Thud and Tintac Ping Foo?'

'Well, of course you can't, as long as the question is only rhetorical,' admitted Omar Khayyam.

Even as he spoke, the caravans of the wicked Princes arrived in the Market Place, and Small Slave spied Abu Ali's White Charger tied up outside Omar Khayyam's Tent Shop.

'Master! Look!' he crowed to Rubdub Ben Thud. 'There's your rival's White Charger!'

'Peals of thunder! So it is!' cried Rubdub, blinking shortsightedly. 'What shall we do now? Kill him at once, or wait till he comes back to fetch his horse? Or both?'

'Never put all your eggs in one basket,' advised Ping Foo profoundly.

'Meaning what?' asked Rubdub sharply.

'One thing at a time,' counselled Ping Foo.

'Oh?' said Rubdub. 'Then why drag in eggs?'

'I never knew a man so touchy about eggs!' grumbled Ping Foo to the world at large.

'Gentlemen, we digress!' insisted Small Slave. 'What do you want to do with your rival's White Charger?'

'Well, what would *you* do?' parried Rubdub cleverly.

'I'd pinch it!' said Small Slave promptly.

'Give reasons for this,' requested Rubdub formally. 'In full.'

'Your rival', explained Small Slave patiently, 'could hardly expect to be taken seriously if he arrived at Sulkpot Ben Nagnag's house on a donkey!'

Rubdub nudged Ping Foo delightedly.

'Isn't that *exactly* what I just said?' he chortled. 'Put it into effect, Small Slave!'

Meanwhile, Abu Ali and Omar Khayyam were perfecting an ingenious battle-plan of their own.

Abu Ali planned to climb Sulkpot's garden wall, hide himself until Silver Bud came out for her daily walk around the lily pond, and then invite her to escape with him over the garden wall. If he was caught by Sulkpot, however, he was to whistle three times, whereupon Omar Khayyam was to run like smoke for help (if any).

'Now, are we fully agreed?' asked Abu Ali carefully.

'Well, yes, and then again, no,' said Omar Khayyam, always the more cautious of the two. 'Suppose Silver Bud *doesn't* choose to escape over the garden wall with you? – though I'm not for a moment suggesting she might not find the idea very attractive – and suppose Sulkpot *does* catch you? Where will it get you? Into a *large* vat of boiling oil! Take the broad view, Abu Ali! Are you really sure she's *worth* it?'

'Yes, yes! A thousand times yes!' cried Abu Ali.

'Then what are we waiting for?' asked Omar Khayyam. 'Let's go!'

In the street, they stared hard at the baggage donkey for a moment.

'Abu Ali, I don't want to alarm you,' said Omar Khayyam, 'but your horse . . . it's shrunk!'

'Omar Khayyam!' said Abu Ali quickly. 'The Wicked Princes are in town! We haven't a moment to lose! On to the donkey with you!'

'Suppose he objects?' countered Omar Khayyam uncertainly.

'No, no!' returned Abu Ali. 'He loves us! You can see it in his eyes! Now, one-two-three-HUP!'

They both jumped on to the donkey's back, and the donkey sat down, and they both slid off backwards.

'Well, now we know he doesn't love us as much as we thought he did,' said Omar Khayyam, picking himself up and dusting the seat of his pants.

'Perhaps he misunderstood us. We'll try again!' said Abu Ali resolutely.

He caught the donkey by the tail and lifted him back on to his feet.

'This time *you* get on first,' he said to Omar Khayyam, 'and I'll stay here to stop him, if he tries to sit down again!'

'Very well!' said Omar Khayyam, and climbed cautiously on the donkey, which immediately sat down again, this time on Abu Ali.

'Perhaps, after all, we'd get there just as soon by foot,' said Omar Khayyam, when he had helped Abu Ali to his feet.

'No!' said Abu Ali, as soon as he got his breath back. 'I refuse to be beaten! Give me a tack!'

Omar Khayyam gave him a tack.

'Now, *next* time, we both jump on together,' he explained, 'and then hold on like fury! Is that clear?'

'It's tempting providence,' said Omar Khayyam gloomily. 'But it's clear.'

'Right!' said Abu Ali, and stood the tack on the ground, point up, just behind the donkey. 'Ready? One-two-three-HUP!'

Together they jumped on to the donkey's back and hung on like fury. The donkey, laughing quietly to himself, sat down as before; but having reckoned without the tack, he sat down on that.

Like a homing swallow, like a comet in the sky – like a donkey that had just sat down on a tack – he sped down the street, and Abu Ali and Omar Khayyam held on like fury.

Chapter The Fifth

Which Explains How Abu Ali Attempted a Rescue

Every afternoon, just before Silver Bud took her daily walk around the lily pond, Sulkpot Ben Nagnag's special guards marched round the garden armed with large knives and long spears. At every hundred paces – which the Captain of the Guard counted under his breath – a guard was left on duty. Each guard had a whistle, and his orders were to blow first and ask questions later.

A guard catching a suitor in the garden was entitled to two gold pieces and Thursday afternoon off.

Now it so happened that the spot below the wall where Abu Ali was scrambling up was one of the sentry-posts; and the guard on duty there was twice as alert as any of the others, for it was the first time he had ever been put on guard duty, *and he was burning with ambition to catch a suitor*.

This was not for the sake of the two gold pieces, or even the Thursday afternoon off – which he would have to spend by himself in any case – but because he longed for an excuse to blow his shiny new whistle more than he had ever longed to do anything since the day he was born.

His name was Kublai Snoo, and he could wiggle his ears.

Unfortunately it never occurred to Abu Ali to watch out for guards before he jumped off the wall. The awful result was that he landed feet-first on Kublai Snoo and drove him head-first into a bed of variegated hollyhocks.

Deep down inside the hollyhock bed, Kublai Snoo first thought he had caught a suitor; then he thought a suitor had caught *him*; and finally he decided there must have been an eclipse of the sun. He gave a half-hearted wriggle and distinctly felt his legs move, so *then* he assumed that he must have been standing on his head to watch the eclipse when an earthquake had taken him unawares.

Abu Ali, seeing the legs wriggle, was too kind-hearted to leave Kublai Snoo to such a fate, in spite of his being a guard; so after he had given him a brisk tug or two, Kublai Snoo suddenly reappeared right-side-up with his cap jammed over his eyes.

For a minute or two he was content to lie on his back and gaze quietly at the inside of his cap; then his worst fears were confirmed. He heard a strange, sinister voice addressing him.

'If you so much as *sneeze*, you'll go back into the flower bed!' the strange voice hissed fiercely. 'I must warn you that we are the forty thieves, and will stop at nothing! Do you understand?'

'Perfectly,' whispered Kublai Snoo faintly.

'We shall now tie you up and gag you!' continued Abu Ali, sounding as ferocious as he could. 'Or would you sooner we cut you up in pieces?'

'No, I wouldn't!' said Kublai Snoo with a gulp.

'Next question!' growled Abu Ali. 'Do you happen to have a piece of string *and* a handkerchief?'

'In my left trouser pocket,' whispered Kublai Snoo, very nearly in a swoon by now.

Abu Ali searched in Kublai Snoo's left trouser pocket and found both. First he tied Kublai Snoo's hands behind his back with the string.

'Now the gag!' said Abu Ali; and as he tied the handkerchief over Kublai Snoo's mouth, he added: 'Is anyone coming, Pasha Ben Hooli?' and then growled 'NO!' in a deep hoarse voice, to show Kublai Snoo what a lot of the forty thieves were attacking him.

Indeed, so occupied with his task had he become, that he failed to hear a delicate footstep approaching.

'What *are* you doing?' asked a surprised little voice behind him.

Abu Ali looked around quickly, and fell absolutely and everlastingly in love at first sight with Silver Bud, who was gazing at him in wide-eyed bewilderment.

'*Oh!*' sighed Abu Ali, struck almost speechless by her beauty. (And so he should have been, gentle reader. No one, before or since, has *ever* been so beautiful.)

'Why have you tied up Kublai Snoo?' she inquired in a voice that was sweeter than all the song-birds you ever heard trill.

'Because I don't want to be boiled in oil,' answered Abu Ali, still gazing at her in rapturous wonder.

'If you don't want to be boiled in oil,' she said very reasonably, 'what are you doing *here*?'

'I came to seek *you*!' he cried, falling on one knee. 'To serve you with my life, beloved Silver Bud!'

'Oh, dear! That's what it nearly always costs,' sighed Silver Bud regretfully. 'Who are you?'

'My name is Abu Ali,' said Abu Ali devoutly. 'And lowly

though I may appear to you, I have sworn a vow to rescue you from this durance vile!'

'Indeed, though I hardly know you, I see you are *very* brave,' confessed Silver Bud, touched to her tender-hearted heart. 'And also very gallant! I couldn't bear to see you boiled in oil! Please go before they catch you!'

'Never, Silver Bud, fairest of the fair!' cried Abu Ali valiantly, rising to his feet. 'Unless I take you with me!'

'*Now?*' asked Silver Bud. 'This very *minute*?'

'*Now!*' nodded Abu Ali. 'This very *minute*!'

'I'd like nothing better!' said Silver Bud, quite delighted. 'But how?'

'All I have to do', said Abu Ali swiftly, 'is to carry you up *this* side of the wall, and help you climb down Omar Khayyam on the other! Ready?'

'Ready!' cried Silver Bud happily; but she had no sooner placed her tiny foot on the first bough of the tree, when Sulkpot Ben Nagnag came bouncing across the garden with his carpet slippers slapping on his bunioned feet.

'Ho, there, guards!' he was roaring hoarsely. 'Stop them! Stop them, I say! Arrest the scoundrel!'

Guards appeared like magic from every corner, and in less time than it takes to tell, Abu Ali was overpowered, though he fought like a tiger and kicked the Captain four times on the same leg before he was subdued.

'Well, what do *you* have to say?' snarled Sulkpot to Silver Bud. 'Explain yourself, young lady, *if* you can!'

'Well, really, Father!' protested Silver Bud in a voice of pure sweet reason. 'My friend and I were simply going to climb this tree to look at a bird's nest –'

'Enough! No more! Not another word!' bellowed her red-nosed father, directing the bulk of his fury at Abu Ali. 'Who *are* you, creature?' he screamed. 'Don't answer that! You're going to be boiled in oil!'

'He shan't boil him in oil!' cried Silver Bud protectively. 'I *love* him!'

'You WHAT??' cried Abu Ali and Sulkpot Ben Nagnag together, but for very different reasons.

'I love him!' repeated Silver Bud, *quite* fearlessly.

Nobody had noticed Kublai Snoo as yet.

'My ears deceive me!' exploded Sulkpot, now quite beside himself. 'I shall choke, or something! Away with him, guards! And make sure you boil him to a crisp!'

'Stop!' cried Silver Bud, facing Sulkpot with her head held high.

'If you boil him in oil,' she informed her father fearlessly, 'I shall never marry anybody else; not as long as I live! And I mean it! I mean it! I *mean* it!'

Nobody had noticed Kublai Snoo as yet, but the hullabaloo had brought the Wicked Princes Rubdub Ben Thud and Tintac Ping Foo prancing into the garden, and they arrived just in time to hear Silver Bud's impassioned words.

'Can I believe my ears?' asked Tintac Ping Foo in horror.

'The echoes must be playing tricks!' said Rubdub quite aghast.

'Call some more guards!' bellowed Sulkpot Ben Nagnag, completely at a loss. 'Lots more guards! I never *heard* of such a thing! Can you be *defying me*, Daughter?'

'Indeed I can!' Silver Bud assured him. 'I *am*!'

'These are all the guards we have,' said the Captain apologetically. 'There *are* no more!'

'Good grief! It's that Abu Ali person!' screamed Tintac Ping Foo, recognizing him for the first time. 'He's here before us!'

'How *can* he be?' cried Rubdub. 'We stole his horse!'

'What's that?' cried Sulkpot Ben Nagnag swiftly. 'Do you two gentlemen *know* this cut-throat?'

'No we don't!' shrilled the Wicked Princes hastily.

'Then, please accept my apologies for this unseemly confusion!' begged Sulkpot, rapidly pulling himself together from every direction. 'And allow me to present my only daughter, Silver Bud!'

'*My!*' said Ping Foo with a smirk.

'Yum yum!' said Rubdub vulgarly.

'Don't trust them!' Abu Ali called to Silver Bud.

'I won't!' she promised him.

'Guards, I thought I told you to remove that knave!' roared Sulkpot.

'Leave him alone!' countered Silver Bud at once. 'I claim the right to choose the bravest for my husband!'

'Me!' cried Tintac Ping Foo instantly.

'Me!' cried Rubdub Ben Thud, not a second later.

'The only way to find out,' continued Silver Bud firmly, 'is to set all three a difficult task, and I shall wed the winner!'

'I agree!' cried Abu Ali. 'What do *you* say, gentlemen?'

This was met by an unaccountable silence, which Ping Foo finally broke with a small cough.

'You said a difficult task?' he asked uneasily.

'*You* heard!' said Abu Ali pointedly.

Prince Rubdub Ben Thud thrust out his lower lip. 'I refuse to commit myself until I've seen my lawyer!' he said tremulously.

'*There* speaks a coward!' cried Silver Bud in fine scorn.

'No, I'm not!' shouted Rubdub. 'But I've had a cold! My mummie says I'm not to get my feet wet!'

'And *I'm* not allowed to talk to strangers!' chimed in Ping Foo. 'Otherwise, I'd take on *any* old task! *And* win!'

'Father!' said Silver Bud firmly. 'Set the tasks!'

'Ah, the trials and the tribulations of a father!' said Sulkpot self-pityingly. 'You can see that I have no choice, gentlemen,' he added apologetically. 'I'm afraid I must ask you, Prince Tintac Ping Foo, to find and bring back – bring back a – let me see; bring back a – ah, yes – bring back a Magic Carpet!'

'A Magic *Carpet!*' echoed Ping Foo in scandalized tones. 'Whatever *for?*'

'And me?' inquired Rubdub Ben Thud uneasily. 'What do *I* have to bring back?'

Sulkpot Ben Nagnag, never a very imaginative man, thought hard.

'Another Magic Carpet,' he said at last.

'Unfair! Unfair!' squealed Rubdub at once.

'And what about the upstart?' snapped Ping Foo spitefully. 'What's *he* got to bring back?'

'Yes! Make it even *more* impossible!' said Rubdub balefully.

'Don't worry! I will!' promised Sulkpot, scowling horribly at Abu Ali. 'You, creature, will bring back Three Tail Feathers from a Magic Phoenix Bird, which is believed to be quite extinct by those who know!'

'Certainly!' said Abu Ali cheerfully. 'Now may I be released?'

'Yes!' said Silver Bud quickly. 'Release him, guards!'

The guards were glad to.

Still nobody had yet noticed Kublai Snoo.

'Magic Carpet!' snarled Ping Foo to the garden wall. 'I'd like to know where I'm expected to find an idiotic thing like *that*!'

Silver Bud laid her hand gently on Abu Ali's arm.

'I know you'll come back safely,' she said tenderly.

'I will! I promise you I will!' vowed Abu Ali with all his heart.

'Good-bye,' said Silver Bud in a small voice.

'Good-bye,' said Abu Ali, and to avoid any display of unheroic feeling, jumped over the wall at a bound.

Chapter The Sixth

Which Explains How Abu Ali Met a Green Dragon,
and How a Spell Went Wrong

When Samarkand lay far behind him, and both Abu Ali and
the donkey were beginning to feel exceedingly tired and
hot, they came upon a Forest of Tall Trees, stretching away
as far as the eye could see, and no doubt farther, if one but
knew.

They rode straight into the Forest, and soon the donkey
was trotting through wooded glades where the branches
knotted their knuckles together over their heads, and small
streams rippled out from behind bushes and rippled back
underneath others, and all was quiet and peaceful.

Then they came to a clearing in the Forest, and there in
the clearing, dancing about and not noticing them as yet,
was a huge, horned, scaly, scowly, nozzle-nosed, claw-
hammered, gaggle-toothed, people-hating, smoke-snorting,
fire-eating, flame-throwing, penulticarnivorous, bright
green Dragon.

Well, the donkey was so paralysed by the spectacle that it
stood rooted to the spot, and Abu Ali was powerless to
make it turn and run.

He simply had to sit there till the Dragon did a
particularly complicated hop-skip-and-turn which brought
him face to face with them. At once he switched off his
dance in mid-sizzle, leaned his spiky elbow against a
convenient tree, and surveyed them intently with his head
on one side.

'You'll forgive me, I'm sure,' said the Green Dragon in
his best party manners, 'but I don't recall the previous
pleasure of your acquaintance! Stranger in these parts?'

'Yes,' said Abu Ali, 'and what is more, lost!'

'Lost, ha?' said the Dragon, with a great show of sympathetic concern. 'Imagine that! Still, that's the way it goes! Here today, and gone tomorrow!' He smiled hard at the donkey, and the donkey dropped its ears uneasily.

'I'm searching,' explained Abu Ali, feeling anxious for the donkey, 'for the Magic Phoenix Birds; and any information you might be kind enough to supply –'

'The Magic Phoenix Birds?' interrupted the Green Dragon expansively. 'I know *exactly* where you'll find them!' And here he eyed the donkey again, and was noticed by Abu Ali to lick his lips with his long heliotrope tongue.

'Then would you direct me to them?' asked Abu Ali. 'If it's not too much to ask?'

'No, no! *Indeed* it's not too much to ask!' the Green Dragon assured him warmly. 'It's the *least* I can do in return!'

'In return for what?' asked Abu Ali.

'In return for eating your donkey with a lettuce salad, tomato sliced thin!' said the Green Dragon, as bland as a beadle.

'Never!' cried Abu Ali resolutely. 'He's as tough as leather!'

'To you, yes,' the Green Dragon agreed. 'To a Green Dragon, tasty and toothsome, tender and plump! And this too must be borne in mind, good sir; if I don't eat your donkey, I'll jolly well eat *you*!'

'Be that as it may,' parried Abu Ali bravely, 'and supposing I *do* give you my donkey, how do I know you'll still keep your word, once you've eaten him?'

'That's a chance we'll all have to take,' said the Green Dragon airily.

Abu Ali reluctantly dismounted.

'Very well,' he said. 'First tell me where I'll find the Magic Phoenix Birds!'

'Nobody knows,' said the Green Dragon blithely, 'so why ask *me*?'

'That's cheating!' cried Abu Ali hotly, and slapped the donkey so hard that it gave one terrified grunt and galloped away like a streak of greased lightning.

'That's *my* property!' gasped the Green Dragon, aghast. 'Give him back!'

'How? That's the last either of us will ever see of *him*!' answered Abu Ali.

'Yes, I know it is!' howled the Green Dragon. 'And I'm *furious*, simply *furious*! In fact,' snarled the Green Dragon, 'I'm *nearly* too furious to eat you instead! *Nearly*!' hissed the Green Dragon. 'But not *quite*! So bid farewell to this empty world of shallow pomp, because HERE I COME!'

He gave a top-heavy pounce, but Abu Ali skipped neatly behind a tree, and the Dragon bumped his head against a knot in the tree trunk and bent one of his horns.

'*Oooh! Ahh! Ouch!*' screamed the Green Dragon in pain.

'Serves you right!' called Abu Ali. 'Now stand aside and let me pass! Unless you want to bend the *other* horn.'

The Green Dragon merely turned his head away and began to whistle off-handedly.

Abu Ali was smart enough to remain where he was. After a long pause, the Green Dragon looked back in his direction.

'Well, I never, did you ever!' he exclaimed in bored surprise. 'You're not still here? I thought you'd gone *ages* ago!'

'No, you didn't!' answered Abu Ali.

'If you come out from behind that tree, I'll boil a kettle on my nose, and we'll all have tea!' offered the Dragon sociably.

'I'm not thirsty,' said Abu Ali.

'Scorpions and centipedes!' snarled the Dragon in fulminous fury, and made another pounce. 'I'll teach you to make me look undignified! Come *here*!' He made another pounce at Abu Ali, and caught his claw in a root, which sat him back on his tail with an echoing thud.

'You realize that we can keep this up indefinitely?' asked Abu Ali from the other side of the tree. '*I'll* stop, if *you* will!'

The Green Dragon sat down, nursing his tail with one claw and rubbing his bent horn with the other.

'You needn't think you'll get away!' he warned Abu Ali nastily. 'Because you *won't*! The *second* you come out from behind that tree, I'll have you down in two gulps! *One* gulp! I'm *furious*!'

Abu Ali leaned against his side of the tree-trunk and summed up the situation. There was no doubt that the Green Dragon meant *exactly* what he said. It was just a question of time before he ate Abu Ali with a lettuce salad, tomato sliced thin.

Only one source of help remained to him. The *one* rub of the Magic Lamp allowed him by Abdul.

Abu Ali peeped around the tree.

The Green Dragon was still rubbing his foot and his bent horn, but he was watching Abu Ali intently.

'Hey there, Green Dragon! Do you know what this is?' asked Abu Ali, holding up the Lamp.

The Green Dragon surveyed it disinterestedly.

'Well, goodie goodie!' he said sarcastically. 'You've brought your own gravy!'

'This,' Abu Ali informed him impressively, 'is not a gravy-boat. It is the Magic Lamp! I have only to give it one rub, and there will be an awful rumble of thunder, the ground will split open, and a large and terrible Djinn will appear in a cloud of green smoke!'

The Green Dragon breathed on his claw, and then buffed it nonchalantly against his scales.

'Pardon me if I don't smile, I have a chipped lip!' he said sarcastically.

'I'll prove it!' declared Abu Ali stoutly. 'One! Two! –'

'*One* moment,' the Green Dragon interrupted rudely. 'It's only fair to tell you that I'm not being fooled by that old lamp! Instead of wasting my valuable time, why don't you act like a man and come out from behind that tree –'

'*Three!*' cried Abu Ali, and rubbed the Lamp.

For a moment the Dragon looked slightly uneasy; but when nothing happened to disturb the peaceful silence of the Forest, he relaxed again.

'Well? One, two, three *what*?' he jeered.

'Just you wait and see!' Abu Ali promised him imposingly.

The silence remained undisturbed.

Abu Ali gave the Lamp another brisk rub.

'Try blowing down it!' suggested the Green Dragon disrespectfully.

The silence returned; but alas, gentle reader, Abu Ali had been so taken aback by the failure of the Lamp that he forgot to keep his peepers open. So when the Green Dragon suddenly pounced, he was just a moment too late to dodge. Before he knew it, he found himself pinned to the ground by ten sharp green claws.

'*Whoops!*' hallooed the Dragon triumphantly. '*Gotcha!* How shall I start? Shall I bite off your head, or start at the toes and nibble you hither and yon?'

But the mocking words were no sooner out of his jaws than a loud burst of thunder belatedly shook the air, and the Green Dragon saw the ground slowly splitting open behind him. Next, a ball of green smoke shot up through the crack in the ground and hovered over the Green Dragon's head.

'Good Old Abdul!' cheered Abu Ali weakly. 'Just in time!'

'Ow, wow, *wow*!' howled the Dragon, executing a perfect somersault from sheer cowardice. He then tore away into the Forest as fast as his legs could carry him; never to be heard from again, not even by postcard.

Abu Ali sat up.

'Thank you, Abdul!' he said gratefully to the Green Cloud bobbing in the air above him.

The Green Cloud was behaving in a most peculiar manner, however; as if a great struggle was going on inside it; so Abu Ali sat down and waited expectantly for a while.

'Is that you, Abdul?' he inquired at last.

'I won't be a moment,' answered the Cloud in a worried voice. 'Something – seems – to have gone – wrong here – but – I'll be done in a jiffy – *Bother!*'

The Cloud gave a sudden lurch sideways, turned upside-down, and then descended to earth with a bump; and a voice that wasn't Abdul's said: 'Oooch!' very painfully.

Then the green smoke slowly faded to reveal a small, round, fat, fourteen-carat, rueful, green-hued Djinn seated on the grass, looking more than slightly dazed.

Abu Ali stared at him in blank surprise.

'*Who are you?*' he asked at last.

'Boomalakka Wee,' said the Small Djinn dejectedly.

'Then what happened to Abdul?' inquired Abu Ali.

'Father was busy, so I came instead,' replied the Small Djinn apologetically, and looked around him for a moment or two.

'Well, well; so this is earth,' he mused, slightly disappointed. 'I was told there was more of it. You may have noticed I had a little trouble with that cloud. Answering the Lamp's a lot more tricky than it looks. But I think I may safely say I have mastered it, so all is well; and you can ask what thou wilt and I shall obey!'

'That's more than kind of you,' answered Abu Ali, 'but my request has already been granted!'

'Oh?' inquired Boomalakka swiftly. 'By whom?'

'You!' said Abu Ali. 'I was about to be eaten by the Green Dragon you scared away. While you were still up in the cloud, this was.'

'Oh, good!' said Boomalakka Wee, cheering up at once. 'I'm better at it than I thought! Well, now that I *am* here, can I be of any other assistance?'

'Well, yes, if it's not too much to ask. I could use another donkey,' Abu Ali confessed.

'A donkey?' repeated Boomalakka Wee efficiently. 'Nothing easier! Just watch me carefully!' He rubbed his fingertips together. 'Presto! One donkey!'

A moment or two passed uneventfully.

'That's funny!' said Boomalakka Wee, wrinkling his brow. 'By rights there ought to be a donkey here!'

'Try again,' suggested Abu Ali. 'You know how stubborn donkeys are!'

'This one, especially!' agreed Boomalakka Wee, and

rubbed his fingertips together again. 'Presto! A donkey!' he repeated, but rather less confidently.

This time there was a noise that sounded like *chug*, and a little puff of dust bounced up off the ground.

Boomalakka's chest swelled triumphantly.

'There you are, you see?' he said, his confidence restored. 'I *knew* I could do it!'

They bent over and looked.

'But isn't that a mouse?' asked Abu Ali.

'It *can't* be!' said Boomalakka Wee.

'I rather think it is,' said Abu Ali.

Boomalakka Wee examined it minutely.

'Yes,' he admitted at last, in a crestfallen voice. 'It *is* a mouse! But it's not what I *ordered*! I *ordered* a donkey! You *heard* me!'

'I did indeed,' agreed Abu Ali.

' "Presto! A donkey!" I said.'

'Your exact words.'

'Exactly! My exact words! And now this mouse!'

'Never mind. Try again,' said Abu Ali encouragingly.

'Well, I would,' confessed Boomalakka Wee, 'but the thing

is, if we *were* going to get a donkey, we'd have got it the first time, or not at all!'

'Am I to assume that you won't be needing me?' inquired the Mouse with *icy* politeness.

'You are. We won't,' affirmed Boomalakka Wee.

'Then, if it's not asking too much, would you be kind enough to repatriate me?' requested the Mouse, still *icily* polite.

'Willingly,' said Boomalakka Wee, rubbing his fingertips together. 'Presto! No more Mouse!' he said.

They all looked at each other in silence.

'I'm still here,' said the Mouse at last, with a touch of asperity.

Boomalakka Wee turned to Abu Ali.

'Tell me, Master,' he said earnestly. 'Does it *have* to be a donkey? I mean, if it came to a pinch, could you make do with a Mouse instead?'

'I'm afraid not,' said Abu Ali regretfully.

'So I should hope!' exclaimed the Mouse tartly. 'Make do, indeed! Glory Ducketts, it's not as if I *wanted* to come, in the first place! Some people – I mention no names, but watch where my eyes rest – might save law-abiding mice a deal of needless inconvenience if they took the trouble to get their spells right!'

'The spell *was* right!' retorted Boomalakka Wee hotly. 'Except that I ordered a donkey.'

'I must be rather dense,' said the Mouse with mounting truculence. 'May we take it one step at a time? The spell was right, except that you ordered a donkey. And what did you get? You got a mouse. So *somebody* blundered. It can't possibly be *you*. So, I suppose it's *me*, for not being a donkey?'

'I didn't say that!' returned Boomalakka Wee swiftly. 'But what I *do* say now is that I've known mice who knew their place, and I've known mice who didn't; and the mice I admire least are the mice who think they're ever so bright and witty!'

'To which type do you infer that I belong?' demanded the Mouse disrespectfully.

'If the cap fits, wear it!' snapped Boomalakka Wee.

'Gentlemen, gentlemen,' Abu Ali restrained them peaceably.

'Gentlemen?' snapped the Mouse, rounding on Abu Ali. 'I'd have thought *you'd* have known better! Can't you tell a lady when you see one?'

'I *beg* your pardon, Ma'am,' said Abu Ali hastily.

'Granted as soon as asked,' the Mouse conceded in a slightly mollified voice. 'And now may I go home? I have friends who will become anxious!'

'Certainly!' replied Abu Ali gallantly. 'Send the lady home at once, Boomalakka Wee!'

'I will as soon as I can get a word in edgeways,' said Boomalakka Wee sulkily, and made the magic pass again.

Nothing happened that hadn't happened before – which was nothing – and Boomalakka Wee blushed bright green with annoyance.

'I can't think *why* it doesn't work!' he said disconsolately. 'I've watched Father often enough!'

The Mouse gave a rather hollow laugh.

'It's come to a *pretty* pass, I *must* say,' she declared to the world at large, 'when a lady has to start life afresh in a strange land, without so much as a *word* of warning or a *crumb* of cheese!'

'I suggest,' said Abu Ali helpfully to Boomalakka Wee, 'that *you* go back and ask Abdul to oblige the lady.'

Boomalakka Wee brightened.

'Of course, yes!' he said, jumping up.

'How,' inquired the Mouse disinterestedly, 'do *you* propose to contact Abdul, when you can't even budge *me*?'

Boomalakka Wee looked daggers at her and stamped on the ground with one foot.

'Going *Down*!' he cried ringingly.

Nothing happened. Nothing whatever.

'So now,' said the Mouse with a touch of morbid satisfaction, '*no one* can get back. We're all here for ever. What fun. Tra-la-la. But, if ever I *do* get back,' she added pugnaciously, 'someone will answer for this! I mention no names, but watch where my eyes rest!'

'Wait,' said Abu Ali soothingly. 'I have the solution. It's very simple. *I'll* rub the Lamp myself. Abdul's bound to answer *me*!'

'No,' said Boomalakka Wee in a small, sad voice. 'This pushy Mouse is right. Abdul won't answer you. The Lamp only works for one Djinn at a time; and as *I* can't get *back*, Father can't get *here*!'

'To sum up,' said Abu Ali with little or no reproach, 'we are lost in the middle of a Forest. We have no means of getting out except by foot. And we may run across a Green Dragon any moment now. Otherwise, I never felt better!'

'Indeed, it even has a bright side,' agreed the Mouse, eyeing Boomalakka Wee expressively. 'You could well say that you lost a donkey, only to gain an even bigger one.'

Chapter The Seventh

*Which Reveals the Awful Villainy of the Wicked Princes
Over a Magic Carpet*

Over the baking, bleaching, brutally blistering Arabian
Desert rode the Wicked Prince Tintac Ping Foo and his
retinue; and the sun beat down, and the dust blew about,
and the camels coughed, and the Wicked Prince Tintac Ping
Foo was in one of his terrible tantrums, for the sand had got
up his nose, which is more than a man can stand.

Hot as he was, however; and angry as he was; the Wicked
Prince Tintac Ping Foo was still able to feel pleased with
himself. Why? Because he had found out through his spies
that in the *exact centre* of the Arabian Desert was *the only
Magic Carpet Shop left in the world*.

He was doubly pleased with himself for having *then*
arranged for *his* spies to tell the spies of the Wicked Prince
Rubdub Ben Thud that the shop was in the middle of the
Sahara Desert; and he was triply pleased with himself
because the last spectacle to meet his eyes as he left
Samarkand had been the Wicked Prince Rubdub Ben Thud
hurriedly setting off for the *Sahara* Desert; which, apart
from being an unbelievably long way off, had no Carpet
Shops *whatsoever*.

Oh, gentle reader, with what triumph did he ride towards
that oasis! And as he entered it from the *right* side, with
what triumph did the Wicked Prince Rubdub Ben Thud
enter it from the *left* side; so that they all met slap in the
middle, right outside the only shop left in the world that
sold Magic Carpets.

The Wicked Prince Rubdub Ben Thud leaned out of his
litter with a smug smile.

'Coo-ee! *I* see you!' he trilled to the Wicked Prince Tintac Ping Foo. 'Fancy meeting *you* here!'

The Wicked Prince Tintac Ping Foo's face went pure white.

'Oh, *no*! It's not *true*!' he groaned, and his teeth chattered like magpies. 'It's a mirage! An optical illusion! Astigmatism! Convergent Strabismus! I can't stand it! I shall have to scream!'

'Come, come! Not in front of the servants!' Rubdub jollied him gaily.

'*How did you get here?*' Ping Foo breathed hoarsely.

'In a litter!' giggled Rubdub. 'My, my, Ping Foo, I was hard put to keep a straight face when you told my spies that this Carpet Shop was in the *Sahara* Desert! And when you thought I *believed* you, a very hearty laugh was had by all! A very *hearty* laugh!'

'This means war!' roared Ping Foo. 'We will fight it out, here and now, till one of us falls, never to rise again!'

'Fally-diddle-di-do!' answered Rubdub in the best of tempers. 'We'll do nothing so footle! Pull yourself together, Ping Foo! I've as much right to buy a carpet here as you have, haven't I?'

Now this was so amiably said that, if only to save face,

Tintac Ping Foo had to pretend he agreed. Side by side, avoiding each other's eye, the Wicked Princes pranced into the Carpet Shop.

Not unnaturally for a Carpet Shop, there was a wide variety of carpets on display inside, of every sort and size and colour; but none of them looked particularly Magic. Nor was there anyone behind the counter; so the Wicked Prince Tintac Ping Foo rapped on it sharply with his knuckles.

'Really!' said Rubdub severely. 'The service here is terrible! Bang on the counter again, Ping Foo!'

'Bang on it yourself!' answered Ping Foo tartly, having banged on it harder than he meant to.

Rubdub clapped his hands together instead.

'Ho, there!' he called loudly. 'Will somebody kindly sell us a carpet before we leave in a huff?'

At these words the curtains in the back of the shop parted, and Aladdin's Wicked Uncle Abanazar hurried out.

You recall, gentle readers, that he had been banished to Persia for his bad behaviour in Peking? Well, the Persians had banished him too; and here he was, rather gone to seed.

'What's that?' he cried pathetically. 'Pardon me, gentlemen! I thought at first you were just a couple of camel drivers! They never buy a thing – just mess the place up and waste my time! Pray sit! I have an *exquisite* line here in Persian carpets, in three convenient sizes, and with every order of a thousand gold pieces, we give away *absolutely free* a special doormat with MOTHER on it in pink wool! It doesn't pay us, but we want the goodwill of the customer above all else! You know our motto? You don't? "The Customer Is Always Right!" That's our motto, gentlemen! And if you don't like your carpet; why, all you have to do is bring it back and we'll change it – we'll be *glad* to change it! It's all part of the Wishwash Ben Ragbag Carpet Company's policy for bigger and better customers, because – as we say in our motto – the Customer Is Always Right, which is why we give away the doormat free –'

'*Desist!*' squealed the Wicked Prince Tintac Ping Foo in a frenzy. 'I came here to buy a Magic Carpet! One that flies! Show me one!'

'And show me, too!' added Rubdub Ben Thud loudly. 'And be sure mine's better than the one you show *him*!'

'I want the finest you have in the shop!' Tintac Ping Foo put in quickly. 'Expense is no object! Serve this portly pumpkin second! *I* asked first!'

'You did not!' said Rubdub fiercely. 'We both asked together; but *I* have a lovable personality, so of *course* he'll serve me first!'

'Well, gentlemen,' began Abanazar awkwardly, 'you've put me in a rather embarrassing position –'

'Stop that mindless jabbering and sell me my Magic Carpet!' ordered Tintac Ping Foo imperiously.

'The fellow was addressing *me*, Ping Foo!' said Rubdub furiously. 'What *manners*!'

'The point is –' Abanazar continued regretfully.

'Never you mind about my manners!' hissed Tintac Ping

Foo to Rubdub Ben Thud sibilantly. 'I shall be served first; so sucks boo!'

'But, gentlemen!' quavered Abanazar tearfully. 'Will you *listen* to me? I'm trying to tell you that *all* I have is the *only* Magic Carpet left in the world!'

'The *what*?' asked Tintac Ping Foo in a horrified gasp.

'*The only who in the world?*' echoed Rubdub Ben Thud in an even more horrified gasp.

'I really can't *tell* you how sorry I am!' mourned Abanazar. 'But the only Magic Carpet left in the world is a Turkish eight-by-ten in brown and white, and it sells for nine-hundred-and-ninety-nine-and-a-half gold pieces!'

'*I'll take it!*' shrieked both the Wicked Princes together, scrambling madly for their purses.

'*Don't sell it to him!*' screamed Tintac Ping Foo, counting out his gold pieces so rapidly that half of them fell to the floor. '*It's mine! It's mine!*'

'*It's not! It's mine!*' screamed Rubdub Ben Thud. '*Get away, Ping Foo; you thief, you!*'

Abanazar stood gazing at them with his mouth open, wishing he had asked twice as much for the Magic Carpet; but after a moment or two, it began to dawn on him that Rubdub Ben Thud's purse, full of gold as it was, didn't hold nine-hundred-and-ninety-nine-and-a-half gold pieces.

As this had also begun to dawn on Ben Thud, he began to count more slowly, and his blood pressure began returning to normal.

Then he noticed that Tintac Ping Foo was counting more slowly too, and had an equally peaky look on his face.

'How many gold pieces do you have in your purse, Foo?' asked Rubdub at last, in a quavering voice.

Tintac Ping Foo glared at Rubdub with jealous loathing.

'Five hundred,' he admitted with poor grace. 'So *you* win, Thud! Go ahead and buy your old carpet, and I hope you roll off it when it's up very high!'

Rubdub shook his head almost soulfully.

'No,' he said. 'I don't win. All *I* have is five hundred gold pieces.'

'Can I interest you gentlemen in two other carpets?' asked Abanazar quickly. 'I have two Bokhara rugs for four-hundred-and-ninety-nine-and-a-half gold pieces each! Of course, we can't guarantee any Magic for *that* price, but you still get the free doormat with MOTHER on it in pink wool, and you'd *laugh* if you knew what a small profit we make on the sale –'

'Will you be *quiet*?' snarled Tintac Ping Foo. 'I'm trying to *think*!'

'I've *thought*,' remarked Rubdub Ben Thud deflatedly, and sat down on a pile of the free doormats with MOTHER picked out in pink wool.

Small Slave, who had been quietly watching every move, now stepped forward.

'Do not despair, Your Highness,' he murmured respect-fully. 'If this is indeed the only Magic Carpet left in the world, Sulkpot Ben Nagnag unknowingly set you both an impossible task.'

'Well, we both know *that*!' snapped Rubdub irritably.

'Yes, tell us something we *didn't* know!' snapped Ping Foo.

'If you *both* buy this carpet,' said Small Slave patiently, 'and fly back on it together, you will have fulfilled *your* parts of the bargain, and Silver Bud will have to choose between you!'

'My very words!' agreed Rubdub.

'Here's *my* five hundred! Now that we're flying back by carpet, we'll get to Samarkand *long* before that stuck-up Abu Ali! Kadoo, kadunk; how *clever* of me to have thought of it in time!'

Without further ado, the Wicked Princes unrolled the Magic Carpet outside the Carpet Shop in the Arabian Desert.

'Don't you *dare* get on before me, Thud!' called the Wicked Prince Tintac Ping Foo excitedly. 'We both get on together! Are you ready? *One – two – three!'*

They both minced on to the Magic Carpet.

'Take us, Carpet,' pronounced Ping Foo solemnly, *'to the House of Sulkpot Ben Nagnag!'*

They braced themselves expectantly, but the Carpet appeared not to have heard.

'It's in Samarkand, Carpet!' added Ping Foo impatiently. 'Near the Market Place! We'll tell you where to stop!'

The Carpet never so much as fluttered.

'That's an *order* you silly Carpet!' said Rubdub crossly. 'Take us there at *once*!'

There was a faint twitch at one corner of the Carpet.

Ping Foo's face began to redden. 'Ben Thud!' he said through his teeth. 'I believe we've been sold another pup! *Hey, Shopkeeper!'*

Abanazar shuffled out of the shop.

'What sort of Magic Carpet do you call this?' demanded Ping Foo indignantly. 'I thought you said it flew?'

'So it does!' returned Abanazar stoutly. 'I had it out this morning, and it flew *beautifully*!'

'Then why doesn't it fly *now*?' snarled Ping Foo.

'Because there's too much weight on it!' answered Abanazar bluntly.

'I demand an immediate apology!' ordered Rubdub hotly.

'Well, if you gentlemen will step off for a moment,' said Abanazar, 'I'll prove it!'

The Wicked Princes eyed each other mistrustfully, but they dutifully counted *One – Two – Three* and stepped off together.

Abanazar squatted himself calmly on the middle of the Carpet.

'Once round the house, please, Carpet,' was all he said.

Right under the disgruntled noses of the two Wicked Princes, the Magic Carpet rose gracefully into the air, sailed effortlessly round the Carpet Shop, and came lightly down to earth again.

'There!' said Abanazar. 'What did I tell you?'

The Wicked Princes looked at each other with absolute loathing.

'*One* of us', said Ping Foo primly and pointedly, 'has got to go back to Samarkand in an old-fashioned hammock!'

Rubdub Ben Thud said nothing, but he looked *blisters*.

'Well?' prodded Ping Foo. 'What are you waiting for, Thud? I'd start now, if I were you!'

'Yes, I think I will. Ta-ta, Ping Foo,' said Rubdub with deceptive meekness; and then suddenly, without *any* warning whatever, he kicked Ping Foo hard on his shin; and as soon as Ping Foo had hopped away on one leg, Rubdub jumped swiftly back on to the Carpet.

'Take me to the Shinpot of Nagnag Ben House, Carpet!' he shouted quickly. 'No, no! I mean to the House of Nagsulk Ben Pot! – No, no! I mean to the Potpot of Sulkhouse Ben, *Ouch*!'

For by now Ping Foo had *hurled* himself head-first at Rubdub with such frenzy that the desert shook with their grunts and groans and wails and screams and many an unkind word.

Chapter The Eighth

Which Explains How Abu Ali Found the Button-Nosed Tortoise and a Great Deal More Trouble as Well

Night had fallen over the Arabian Desert.

It was a particularly stark, dark, pitch-black night, and the air was cool and growing cooler every minute, which meant that before long it would be downright brisk; and there sat Abu Ali, Boomalakka Wee and the Mouse, entirely surrounded by sand; and Boomalakka Wee was shivering and blowing on his fingers.

'If only the *Moon* would come out!' he kept repeating mournfully.

'Personally,' announced the Mouse austerely, sitting on her paws to keep them warm, 'I don't care *what* the moon decides to do! I'm homesick, I miss my friends, and I'm *aching* for a scrap of toasted cheese!'

'Oh, come; cheer up!' said Abu Ali kindly. 'Things are bound to get better!'

'Who cares if they do? They'll only get worse again!' returned the Mouse, quite inconsolable, and two sedate tears rolled down her nose.

'You're not the only pebble on the beach!' said Boomalakka Wee pathetically. 'I'm homesick too!'

'*You* deserve to be!' the Mouse informed him tensely. 'If it hadn't been for *you* –! Oh, I don't know why I bother! Water off a duck's back! Though I doubt that even a backward duck would answer a Lamp it didn't know how to answer; and then start spells it didn't know how to finish –!'

She broke off suddenly, and patted the ground in a mystified manner with her paw.

'Abu Ali!' she said with all due caution. 'Something strange and peculiar is taking place!'

'What kind of something?' asked Abu Ali, straining his eyes in the dark.

'I don't know,' said the Mouse, now openly alarmed. 'But I have an unaccountable conviction that I'm sitting on green grass!'

'That's yet *another* bee in your bonnet!' said Boomalakka Wee with regrettable vulgarity.

Abu Ali patted the ground beside him, and instead of patting sand, he found that *he* was patting green grass.

'In that case, I have a bee in *my* bonnet too!' he said. 'Because I'*m* also sitting on green grass! My, how quickly it grew!'

'And now I smell flowers!' announced the Mouse.

'Sheer hallucinootions!' said Boomalakka Wee disrespectfully.

'No; I too smell flowers!' said Abu Ali. 'Is it possible that we've been walking in our sleep? No, it can't be! We haven't gone to sleep yet!'

'Then why are we no longer where we were, but elsewhere?' asked the Mouse with deep foreboding.

'We're not elsewhere!' said Boomalakka Wee. 'Because why? Because *I* don't smell any flowers, and I'*m* not sitting on green grass!'

But the brave words were no sooner out of his mouth, than he gave a heartfelt wail of alarm.

'Abu Ali! I take it all back!' he cried remorsefully. 'I'm sitting on a stone, and there's running water all around me!'

'There he goes again, anything for attention!' said the Mouse in disapproval.

'I'm telling you the *truth*!' Boomalakka Wee insisted tearfully. 'AH – H – H – CHOO!'

His sneeze was followed by an enormous splash, then a bubbling noise, and then a very damp voice cried: '*Glub – glub – ubble – glug – help! I'm drowning.*'

'What a commotion!' said the Mouse primly. 'Anyone who didn't know you would think you were in real water!'

'I am!' wailed Boomalakka Wee in tears.

'Whereabouts are you?' shouted Abu Ali. 'Swim towards me, and I'll help you out!'

'Unless you've sunk!' added the Mouse practically.

'Boomalakka Wee! You haven't sunk, have you?' called Abu Ali anxiously.

'Yes! Twice!' answered Boomalakka Wee's voice dolefully, coming nearer. 'And I'm frozen stiff!'

'If only the moon would come out!' groaned Abu Ali. 'At least we could *see* what he fell in!'

Now they heard Boomalakka Wee squelch on to a patch of dry land near by.

'A fine thing!' he complained dispiritedly. 'I sit down on hot sand in the middle of a desert, and the next thing I know, I'm up to my neck in an ice-cold torrent! I'd like it explained, that's all!'

'Look!' cried Abu Ali in relief. 'The moon at last!'

He had barely spoken when a pale yellow glow came stealing through the clouds, and they found themselves on the bank of a bubbling stream, in the middle of a perfectly *delightful* wood.

'It's a wood!' said Abu Ali immediately.

'So it is!' agreed the Mouse. 'It's a wood!'

Boomalakka Wee frowned and looked about him.

'It's a w-w-wood,' he said begrudgingly, 'and I'd like *that* explained, too!'

'Why, of course!' Abu Ali burst out excitedly. 'Why didn't we realize it at once? Boomalakka Wee! Mouse! *We're in the Land of Green Ginger!*'

'Who? Me?' asked Boomalakka Wee blankly.

'Prove it!' demanded the Mouse.

'We happened to be sitting on the particular piece of the Arabian Desert that it chose to settle on!' explained Abu Ali.

'An interesting theory,' granted the Mouse, not budging an inch, 'but if it settled *on* us, why aren't we *underneath* it instead of *on top* of it?'

'Ah,' said Abu Ali profoundly. 'Well, yes. But then again, why bother?'

'We have troubles enough!' the Mouse agreed wholeheartedly.

The moon was as bright as a new cheese now, and they could see every detail of the Land of Green Ginger quite clearly. It was sprinkled with ginger trees laden down with branch upon branch of sparkling sugar-coated green ginger; and big bright beauteous flowers grew out of the soft velvety grass, and water-lilies floated on a cheerful little hubble-bubbling stream. It was all charmingly rural. No bits of paper, no empty bottles, no initials carved on the tree-trunks. You cannot imagine such natural wonders, gentle reader; you must simply take my word for it.

'There's not a moment to be lost!' cried Abu Ali. 'We must find the Magic Phoenix Birds before the night's an hour older!'

'Not me!' announced Boomalakka Wee. 'I've had enough! And I always spoil it for everyone else anyway!'

'Well, *you* said it; *we* didn't!' said the Mouse briskly. 'Good-bye, Wee!'

'Good-bye!' said Wee haughtily.

But Abu Ali and the Mouse had no sooner set off, than a loud whirring noise broke out directly above Boomalakka Wee's head, and he cried, 'Woo-*oo*! Wait for me!' and belted after them.

Abu Ali was already gazing up at the tree-tops ahead of them.

'I see them!' he whispered. '*Big* birds! The Magic Phoenix Birds! Quick, Boomalakka Wee; hand me my bow-and-arrow! You were carrying it!'

'Was I?' asked Boomalakka Wee in a small voice.

Abu Ali turned around hastily.

'Of course you were! You *insisted* on carrying it! You haven't *lost* it?' he asked desperately.

'Don't be cross with me, Abu Ali. It's at the bottom of the stream,' said Boomalakka Wee dejectedly.

Without a word, Abu Ali caught him by the hand and rushed him back to the stream.

'Whereabouts did you fall in?' he asked quickly. 'Quick! Show me! Here?'

'No, there,' said Boomalakka Wee, pointing. 'No. It was higher up. No; lower down.'

Abu Ali ran along the bank of the stream.

'Here?' he asked anxiously.

'Yes,' said Boomalakka Wee without conviction.

Abu Ali jumped into the stream and began feeling about for the bow-and-arrow.

'Are you *sure* you fell in here?' he asked urgently.

Boomalakka Wee sat down on the bank and hugged his knees disconsolately.

'Not very,' he admitted forlornly. 'One part of a stream's much like another. It was near a rock.'

'The stream's *full* of rocks!' said the Mouse briskly. 'Which rock?'

'*Try* to remember, Boomalakka Wee!' beseeched Abu Ali.

'I *think* it was *that* one,' said Boomalakka Wee, pointing desperately at the first rock he saw.

Abu Ali splashed all around the rock.

'Find anything?' asked the Mouse.

'No,' said Abu Ali.

'I didn't think you would,' said the Mouse.

'It's all my fault!' admitted Boomalakka Wee, on the brink of tears. 'I *do* feel awful, Abu Ali!'

'Cheer up,' said Abu Ali. 'It may have drifted downstream. I'll look,' and he waded downstream until it turned a bend and they could see him no longer.

The Mouse sat down beside Boomalakka Wee.

'Rule One in any emergency!' she said tartly. 'Sit back and leave it to Wee!'

Abu Ali followed the stream till it disappeared under a mossy rock, and then he regretfully decided that his bow-and-arrow was lost for ever.

He waded to the bank, and began squeezing the water out of his clothes.

'My, my! You *are* wet, aren't you?' inquired a dignified but otherwise unfamiliar voice behind him.

Abu Ali spun round quickly. A Large Tortoise was gazing at him inquiringly over a toadstool. And it wore *enormous* tortoiseshell spectacles at the end of its nose, which was shaped like a button.

'Why, it's *you*!' cried Abu Ali delightedly.

'You must be Abu Ali!' replied the Button-Nosed Tortoise with grave courtesy. 'I was beginning to fear we'd never meet! The odds against it were formidable – what with neither of us able to calculate where this erratic *flora et fauna cum laudibus* would decide to settle next! By the way, does that belong to you?' he added, waving his flipper at the bow-and-arrow, which lay on the bank. 'It came floating

past a little while ago, and, having mistaken it for a rare variety of edible asparagus, I retrieved it!'

'I can never thank you enough!' Abu Ali assured him gratefully, picking up the bow-and-arrow. 'But first things first! How do I break your spell?'

'I can answer you in a nutshell,' the Button-Nosed Tortoise replied graciously. 'Even without a nutshell. You observe that *large* water-lily (genus *oblata longata mompara*), in the middle of the stream? Pick it, if you'd be so kind. I'd have done it long ago, but I can't swim,' he added scientifically. 'Once tried. Sank like a stone. Watch out. Deep there!'

'Very!' agreed Abu Ali, once he had resurfaced and emptied the water out of his ears.

Carefully avoiding the rest of the deep hole, he picked the water-lily and waded back to the bank.

'Did I do it right?' he asked anxiously.

'You most certainly did!' the Button-Nosed Tortoise assured him warmly.

'Then why are you still a Button-Nosed Tortoise?' asked Abu Ali in pardonable disappointment.

'The spell works in stages,' explained the Button-Nosed Tortoise benignly. Whereupon he ate the water-lily. 'Tastes terrible,' he added, pulling a face, 'but at dawn tomorrow morning, I'll be myself again! Would you be good enough to call on me just after sunrise?'

'Nothing would give me greater pleasure!' replied Abu Ali courteously.

'Thank you. Good evening,' returned the Tortoise, disappearing into his shell without another word.

Abu Ali hurried back to Boomalakka Wee and the Mouse, who were sitting where he had left them.

'I found the Button-Nosed Tortoise!' he cried in high excitement. 'And I've broken the spell – or shall have, by sunrise!'

'Something attempted, something done', quoted the Mouse with composure, 'has earned a night's repose.'

'Oh, no, it hasn't!' said Abu Ali firmly. 'Not until I get the tail feathers from a Phoenix Bird!'

'Oh, *them*!' said Boomalakka Wee brightly. 'They flew away, quite some time ago!'

'Well, really! You *might* have kept an eye on them!' said Abu Ali with a touch of annoyance, and set off into the wood with his bow-and-arrow. The Mouse pattered after him.

'Cheer up. They can't have gone far. It's not that big a wood,' she said consolingly.

'Shh!' whispered Abu Ali, and she shushed obediently.

'Yoo-hoo! Wait for mee-hee!' yelled Boomalakka Wee in a voice so loud that its echoes met in the middle.

Abu Ali and the Mouse jumped a foot in the air.

'Quiet!' shouted Abu Ali frantically.

'Why?' asked Boomalakka Wee.

'We're stalking Phoenix Birds!' said the Mouse under her breath. 'That is, we *were*, until you bellowed your head off!'

But even as she was speaking, they all heard the whirring sound above their heads again, and *right above them* two

Magic Phoenix Birds began circling curiously, having mistaken Boomalakka Wee's bellowing for the call of the Zanzibar Ostrich in moult.

What do Phoenix Birds look like, gentle reader? They look like blue-and-purple storks, except that they have tufted golden crests on their heads, emerald-green beaks and legs; and they sparkle and glitter like all the precious stones in Aladdin's Cave.

Abu Ali drew his bow-and-arrow taut, aimed carefully, and *plunk-whissht*! his arrow neatly removed three tail feathers from the larger Phoenix Bird.

It gave a shrill, discordant screech, looped the loop, and then dived suddenly down towards him.

'Run!' squeaked the Mouse. 'You've *maddened* him!'

She dived under a ginger bush, where Boomalakka Wee joined her with alacrity.

Abu Ali stood his ground, but he felt a little nervous when the Phoenix Bird alighted in front of him. It was obviously twice his own height, even without stretching.

It stood for a moment just glaring at Abu Ali dangerously; then it half closed one eye in a sinister way, and leaned forward till they stood eyeball to eyeball.

'Did *you* shoot out all three of those feathers?' asked the Phoenix Bird grimly at last.

'Yes,' said Abu Ali bravely.

'On purpose?'

'I'm afraid, yes.'

'Things have come to a sorry state,' said the Phoenix Bird austerely, 'when a law-abiding, self-respecting Phoenix Bird can't venture out of his nest without assault and battery to his tail feathers!'

'It's an outrage!' said the second Phoenix Bird shrilly, alighting beside her spouse. 'Make an example of the dismal ruffian!'

'I'm not a dismal ruffian, ma'am!' Abu Ali assured her earnestly. 'These feathers are vitally necessary to me –'

'I like *that*!' huffed the Phoenix Bird indignantly. 'I suppose they weren't vitally necessary to *me*? I suppose you think I can grow a new tail feather overnight?

He shook with eloquent fury for a moment; then his curiosity got the better of him, and he added in a puzzled voice: '*Why* are they vitally necessary to you? *You're* not a bird!'

'I need them to win the hand of the jeweller's daughter, Silver Bud, whom I love with all my heart and soul!' said Abu Ali with impressive conviction.

'*Ho!*' said the lady Phoenix Bird sharply. 'Then you *knew* they were valuable! That leaves you with no excuse whatever!'

'Oh, I wouldn't go so far as to say *that*, my dear,' said the first Phoenix Bird in a friendlier voice. 'After all, if the young gentleman needs them to win a bride, it hardly comes under the heading of an outrage. Suppose we say no more about it, young fellow-me-lad?'

'That's *exceedingly* generous of you, sir!' began Abu Ali

gratefully; but the lady Phoenix Bird wasn't letting him off as lightly as that.

'*If*,' she informed him haughtily, 'you had approached my husband in a decent and civilized manner, and not shot at him with a bow-and-arrow, we would willingly have *donated* three tail feathers left over from last year's season; and everyone would have been spared a very painful scene!'

'I agree, ma'am,' said Abu Ali humbly. 'I can only tender my profound apologies!'

'Pray don't give it another thought,' said the first Phoenix Bird pleasantly. 'But if you come across any *other* young gentlemen who are after my tail feathers, you might explain that they don't have to use me for target practice! Come along, dear!'

And without more ado, the two Phoenix Birds spread their greeny-blue wings and flew off into the wide blue yonder.

Boomalakka Wee and the Mouse carefully crawled out backwards from under the ginger bush.

'Those birds could give a lot of people I know a lesson in good manners,' said the Mouse, profoundly impressed.

'They could indeed!' agreed Abu Ali, picking up the three tail feathers with loving care. 'Now! First to snatch a wink of sleep; and tomorrow morning we start for Samarkand!'

But, alas, gentle reader, what no one suspected at the moment was that the Wicked Princes, and Abu Ali, and the Land of Green Ginger – although they had started from three separate directions – all had the same destination in common; and *you* know, and *I* know, that this can have only one result.

Whether they liked it or not, they were all bound to meet in the middle.

Chapter The Ninth

*Which Explains How the Wicked Princes Went Back
to Their Old Tricks Again*

The Wicked Princes Tintac Ping Foo and Rubdub Ben Thud
were utterly exhausted. They had been carrying the Magic
Carpet across the Arabian Desert for a whole day, and
neither of them was used to carrying *anything*, let alone a
Magic Carpet that grew steadily heavier as they hobbled
along.

Small wonder, then, that when they saw the Land of
Green Ginger in the distance, they almost squinted with
relief.

'Look! Look!' cried Rubdub Ben Thud. 'An oasis!'

'We must be off our route!' said Small Slave, mystified. 'It
wasn't here the last time we passed!'

'Nonsense!' huffed Rubdub. 'I remember it *perfectly*!'

He looked defiantly at the Wicked Prince Tintac Ping
Foo.

'I suppose *you'll* think I'll try to steal the Carpet, if I
suggest we rest here for the night?' he asked coldly.

'No,' returned Ping Foo wearily, 'because I shall sleep on *my* half of the Carpet!'

'You *would*!' growled Rubdub under his breath. 'A suspicious mind, and not much of it!'

'Would you care to repeat that without a potato in your mouth?' asked Ping Foo superciliously.

'As often as you like!' answered Rubdub. 'I'll be glad to add this, too! If you *weren't* a man with a suspicious mind and not much of it, we wouldn't have had to carry this perishing Carpet all the way to Timbuktoo and back again!'

'I quite agree!' snarled Ping Foo. 'You'd have stolen it before we'd left the Carpet Shop!'

What had made them edgier than usual was the fact that the caravans of the Wicked Princes had reached the edge of the Land of Green Ginger; and Small Slave, who had hurried on ahead, now came running back in a dither.

'Stop!' he hissed to the Wicked Princes. 'Don't advance another *inch*!'

'Why not?' asked Rubdub, suffering instant conniptions. 'Robbers? Dragons? Bogeymen?'

'No! Your rival, Abu Ali!' answered Small Slave swiftly. 'He's here before you! Asleep! And he's no longer alone! He has accomplices with him – a small fat man and a mouse! Both asleep also! Fate has delivered them into our hands, Master! There's nothing for it but!'

'What *ghastly* bad grammar!' cried Ping Foo with a shudder. 'A sentence without syntax is like an egg without salt!'

Rubdub's face turned fiery red.

'There you go again, dragging in eggs!' he said fiercely. 'You *know* I hate the very *mention* of the word!'

'I was referring solely to Small Slave's grammar!' answered Ping Foo testily.

'Pardon my grammar for a moment!' begged Small Slave

urgently. 'If you want to remove your rival for ever from your path, you must act, and act *now*! Put down that Carpet a moment, and come and look!'

'I don't let go of this Carpet,' snarled Ping Foo through his teeth. 'Not for a *second*!'

'Nor me!' snarled Rubdub Ben Thud. 'Not for all the chee in Tina!'

'Then bring it with you!' snapped Small Slave, his patience almost gone. 'Ho, there, guards! Bring some rope!'

'How much rope?' asked the head guard alertly. 'A lot?'

'Enough to tie up Abu Ali, a fat little man, and a mouse! This way, Masters!' he added to the two Wicked Princes. 'And don't make a *sound*, or you'll count your chickens before they're hatched.'

'Here we go with eggs again!' groaned Rubdub tormentedly.

'*Hush!*' implored Small Slave, and the three of them tiptoed cautiously through the ginger trees, followed by the guards with a rope, until they came to the clearing where Abu Ali and Boomalakka Wee and the Mouse were peacefully sleeping.

'Observe them?' hissed Small Slave. '*Keep on tiptoe, guards! – By the right, forward creep! – Bind them!*'

'And be sure the knots are tight!' added Rubdub, retiring discreetly in case the wrong side won.

The guards crept up so stealthily that before Abu Ali and Boomalakka Wee and the Mouse were properly awake, they had been overpowered and pinioned; and to add insult to injury, Small Slave tore three strips off Boomalakka Wee's turban and gagged them.

As soon as they were sure that neither Abu Ali nor Boomalakka Wee nor the Mouse could move or make a sound, the Wicked Princes swaggered up boldly.

'That'll teach you, Abu Ali!' scolded Tintac Ping Foo. 'Long may you rue the day you crossed our paths!'

'We'll remember you to Silver Bud!' Rubdub Ben Thud added sarcastically. 'By the by, have you noticed what we're carrying? It's our Magic Egg – I mean, our Magic *Carpet*! – and we're on our way to Samarkand! Drop us a line when you're not so tied up!'

'Wait!' said Small Slave observantly. 'We ought to take these Magic Feathers too!'

'Ah yes!' agreed Tintac Ping Foo. 'Give them to me, Small Slave! I'll take care of them!'

'Oh, no you won't!' parried Rubdub in a flash. 'Not on

your egg – I mean, not on your *life*, Ping Foo! Small Slave found them, and Small Slave shall keep them until we get to Samarkand!'

Tintac Ping Foo, though tempted, restrained a wild desire to hit Rubdub on the head with his half of the Carpet.

'Very well,' he agreed, pretending not to care. 'We haven't time to argue about omelettes – I mean, trifles! Which is the quickest way out of here?'

'Follow me,' said Small Slave. 'And if I may be so bold, I suggest Your Highnesses spread the Carpet over one of the hardier camels. That way *both* of you can ride on *top* of it; thereby killing two birds with one egg – I mean *stone*!'

'There's no getting away from it,' said Rubdub admiringly. 'You have to admit it. Small Slave has a brilliant egg – I mean *brain*!'

By dawn the next day, the Wicked Princes had ridden at such a gallop that they were already half-way to Samarkand.

They would have been even nearer, except that they were so *exorbitantly heavy*, when added together, that they had to keep changing camels, and this wasted many precious hours.

When the same sun rose, it occurred to Abu Ali, as he lay trussed and helpless, that the Button-Nosed Tortoise's spell should have broken by now.

The hours crept by, however, and the Magician *didn't* come looking for him; so at last Abu Ali had no choice but to presume that the spell *hadn't* been broken after all, and that no help could be expected from that quarter or any other.

He wriggled over on his side and looked for hopeful signs from Boomalakka Wee. Boomalakka Wee showed none, mainly because he had gone to sleep from sheer exasperation; but the Mouse, who was made of sterner

stuff, was busy nibbling the piece of turban that Small Slave had tied around her nose, and had almost nibbled it through, for she had been working on it all night long.

When she was completely free, she scampered over to Abu Ali and set about nibbling the rope round his hands.

Now this was a formidable task for any mouse, for the rope was not only thick and strong; it had been tarred; and tar had *particularly* painful associations for the Mouse, because it recalled to mind a gentleman friend who had run away to sea and never come back, though she still nursed hopes of a letter of apology from him.

As soon as he was free, Abu Ali swept her up in his arms and kissed her on both cheeks.

'Fie!' she protested. 'How ostentatious!' But she blushed delightedly none the less, for no one had kissed her since the gentleman friend had run away to sea, which was *many* years before.

Boomalakka Wee, as soon as Abu Ali released him, sat up with a look of battle in his eye and said: 'Heads will roll! Mark my words! Just wait and see!'

'We have to catch them first!' returned Abu Ali. 'Quick! Follow me!'

But Boomalakka Wee had barely gone a step before he shouted: '*Ouch!*' and then: '*Wouch!*' and wobbled to the ground in a heap.

The Mouse, against her better judgement, turned round and ran back to him.

'Back on your toes, Wee! You'll get left behind again!' she rallied him.

'I can't! It's my legs!' wailed Boomalakka Wee. 'They've gone numb through being tied up so long!'

Abu Ali came racing back towards them at full tilt.

'We can *never* get out of here!' he cried in manly aggravation.

'Of *course* we can! Why ever not?' cried the Mouse.

'Because we're miles up in the air!' lamented Abu Ali. 'The Land of Green Ginger's on its travels again, *and it's going the wrong way!*'

Chapter The Tenth

Which Explains How Sulkpot Ben Nagnag Went Back on His Word

For a moment no one spoke because of the awful blow it was to suddenly find oneself miles up in the air *and* going in the wrong direction. But at last the Mouse broke the silence.

'Well, there's no hurry about getting you back on to your feet; *is* there, Wee?' she said, adding conversationally to Abu Ali, 'Wee's trotters have rather let him down.'

'But, Abu Ali!' exclaimed Boomalakka Wee, unable to meet the crisis with the same fortitude as the Mouse. 'There *must* be *some* way to stop it!'

'Name one!' said Abu Ali. 'No. We're helpless until it decides it wants to land again! If *only* the spell had worked on the Button-Nosed Tortoise! Well; the least I can do is go and look for him!'

'Wait for me!' trilled the Mouse instantly. 'I *hate* to feel I might be missing something!'

She trotted after Abu Ali, leaving a mournful Boomalakka Wee to wish with all his might that he had thought twice about answering the Lamp when Abu Ali rubbed it.

Abu Ali followed the stream to the bend, where he had left the Button-Nosed Tortoise the night before.

There was not the slightest trace of a Button-Nosed Tortoise to be seen; but what they *did* see was a scholarly old gentleman with white whiskers, making notes in a big leather notebook.

'What have we here? Stowaways?' he inquired over the top of his *enormous* spectacles. 'Why; bless my wand and whiskers! It's Abu Ali! What a welcome sight!'

'Then the spell *did* work!' cried Abu Ali in delight, and having explained how urgent it was for him to reach Samarkand while there was still time to save Silver Bud, he earnestly requested the Magician to let them out at the next stop.

'The next stop?' echoed the Magician. 'Bless my wand and whiskers, I'll do more than that! I'll take you right to Samarkand!'

And he had no sooner made a small magic pass in the air, than the Land of Green Ginger banked smoothly, and began flying back the way it had come.

'You see?' chirped the Magician delightedly. 'It's working *perfectly*! You're a fine young lad; and whatever service I can do for you is as good as done! Ask anything – anything!' he added encouragingly.

The Mouse tugged at Abu Ali's slipper.

'Ask him to turn the Wicked Princes into beetles!' she whispered longingly.

'Beetles? Nothing easier!' the Magician assured him willingly. 'You have but to say the word!'

Abu Ali pondered the offer for a moment, for in many ways, it was a tempting one. But at last he shook his head.

'No,' he decided, with only slight reluctance, 'they must be beaten by fair means! I'd sooner you helped Boomalakka Wee and the Mouse. They're extremely anxious to return home; but Boomalakka Wee's spells aren't all they should be!'

'Well, before I say yes or no, I'll have to know what *type* of spell they're under!' advised the Magician cautiously. 'Because once one makes the smallest slip, and *Poof*! – one's a Button-Nosed Tortoise, for instance!'

Without further ado, Abu Ali took him to meet Boomalakka Wee, and as soon as they were properly introduced, they plunged into a long and complicated discussion about spells; in the course of which it became steadily more obvious to Boomalakka Wee that he knew even less about the Magic Lamp and what worked it than he thought he did, which had never been much.

Meanwhile, the Mouse became curiously subdued for a Mouse who was about to be restored to her friends at long last. She showed no interest whatsoever in the debate between Boomalakka Wee and the Magician; which had now become so complicated that it was *miles* over Boomalakka Wee's head.

But at last the Magician nodded sagely and said: 'I think I have diagnosed the problem! Without a doubt, this is a case of a clogged spell!'

'You mean you can unclog it?' chittered Boomalakka Wee, hardly daring to believe his fat little green cars.

'We must not run before we can walk,' replied the Magician carefully. 'The proper procedure for returning a Djinn to his correct postal address is for him to stamp on the ground, which forthwith opens and swallows him. Am I correct so far?'

'Of course, if you say so, Your Honour!' said Boomalakka Wee humbly, not having understood a *word*.

'Then kindly stamp on the ground,' requested the Magician, 'while I watch for possible inaccuracies.'

'I'm afraid his legs are too numb,' began the Mouse protectively.

'Not now they're not!' squeaked Boomalakka Wee excitedly, and stamped hard. 'Look! This is the way I stamped, which is *exactly* how Father always did it; but nothing happens, see? *Nothing!*'

He stamped twice more to remove all doubt.

The Magician closed one eye and concentrated with formidable concentration, and there was absolute quiet in the Land of Green Ginger, except for the soft *swoosh-swoosh* it made as it sailed through the air.

At last the Magician opened his eye and smiled a wise and scientific smile.

'Elementary, my dear Wee,' he said airily, and having paused just long enough to achieve the maximum dramatic effect, he added solemnly: 'You have been stamping with the wrong foot!'

'The wrong –' chittered Boomalakka Wee, and then gulped. 'The wrong f-f-f –' and had to stop and gulp again, because his ears were now singing like crickets.

'That's right,' said the Magician kindly. 'So try stamping with the other foot!'

Without another word (for he could think of none sufficiently auspicious), Boomalakka Wee stamped with his other foot; and it had barely touched the ground before there was a rumble of thunder that made everybody jump, and then the ground split open right under their noses, and Boomalakka Wee began turning into a small, blissful Green Cloud.

'Oh, joy! Good-bye! Good-bye!' he cried in a transport of delight.

'Wee, come back!' called Abu Ali anxiously. 'You're forgetting the Mouse!'

'My goodness, so I am!' exclaimed the Green Cloud apologetically, turning back into Boomalakka Wee at once. 'Come along, Mouse!'

[85]

But to everyone's surprise, the Mouse firmly shook her head.

'What?' asked Boomalakka Wee, amazed. 'You mean you're *not* coming back with me?'

'Come, come, Madam,' warned the Magician. 'That means you may *never* be able to get back!'

'Doubtless,' shrugged the Mouse.

'But what can have changed your mind, at the very last minute?' demanded Abu Ali. 'You've been eating your little heart out to get home!'

'When a lady chooses to change her mind,' said the Mouse with a touch of hauteur, 'a gentleman would consider it no more than her privilege, and not badger her about it. But if you *must* know,' she added, 'it's because I *must* know what happens in the end! So off you go, Wee! And don't forget to write!'

But Boomalakka Wee gazed at the Mouse as if he had been rapped by a falling coconut.

'I have never in my life felt so stupid!' he burst out remorsefully. 'Pardon me while I kick myself!'

He did so, hard.

'Whatever was *that* for?' asked Abu Ali in surprise.

'For thinking only of my silly self in the heat of the moment!' he answered. 'You brought me to my senses in the nick of time, Mouse!'

'Don't tell me *you've* decided not to go home, either?' demanded the Mouse. 'Really! Of all the copycats!'

'Of *course* I won't go home till we *all* know what happens in the end!' vowed Boomalakka Wee resolutely. 'Why, what a fair-weather friend I'd be! And quite apart from every-thing else, Abu Ali, how *ever* would you manage without me?'

'Abu Ali,' observed the Magician, profoundly stirred, 'you are indeed fortunate in possessing two such loyal companions!'

'I can only assure you, Mouse; *and* you, Boomalakka

Wee,' said Abu Ali simply, 'that you have touched me far more deeply than I can say!'

'Oh, pish!' said the Mouse with a blush. 'Let's not make mountains out of cheese-crumbs!'

And as she spoke, the Land of Green Ginger began to tip gently to one side.

'Please take your seats! We're landing!' called the Magician excitedly. 'Doesn't she do it *beautifully*?'

A soft bump then informed them that the Land of Green Ginger had come to rest, so they all stood up and proceeded in an orderly manner to the edge of the clearing.

So accurate was the Land of Green Ginger's sense of direction, gentle reader, that directly facing them were the Gates of Samarkand! And sitting on the ground in front of the gates, gazing in stunned stupefaction at the Land of Green Ginger, was Omar Khayyam.

'Abu Ali,' he requested in uneasy tones, 'would you be kind enough to pinch me?'

Abu Ali obliged.

'Oh, that's bad!' he said with profound misgiving. 'It's still here! Only a moment ago, Abu Ali, I was sitting here without a care in the world – so I thought! – composing a verse, when all of a sudden – *pff!* One moment, wilderness; the next, botanical gardens!'

'You're looking at the one-and-only Land of Green Ginger!' Abu Ali reassured him proudly. 'May I present to you the Magician who made it? And my two faithful companions, Madam Mouse and Boomalakka Wee?'

'How dee doo?' said the Magician.

'How dee doo?' said the Mouse.

'How dee doo?' said Boomalakka Wee.

'So you're *not* an optical illusion!' said Omar Khayyam in vast relief, scrambling to his feet and bowing. 'Allow me to say that I'm delighted to make your various acquaintances!'

On this cordial note the Magician said good-bye all round, re-entered the Land of Green Ginger, and turned its foliaged prow skywards.

And at the precise moment that it disappeared from sight, the Mouse slapped her forehead in vexation.

'Do you know what we forgot to do?' she demanded. 'We forgot to ask for three more Tail Feathers!'

'Now, why couldn't you have thought of that while there was still time?' asked Boomalakka Wee severely.

'Why couldn't *you*?' returned the Mouse.

'Why couldn't I?' said Abu Ali, shouldering full blame. 'Still, we've no time to cry over spilt milk! I must go and supply Sulkpot with an *exact* account of everything that has happened!'

'*Without* the Three Tail Feathers?' asked the Mouse.

'*Without* the Three Tail Feathers!' nodded Abu Ali.

'Wouldn't it be wiser to write him a letter?' suggested Omar Khayyam.

'No, no; he must be bearded in his den!' said Abu Ali.

'Our friend Abu Ali is a stubborn fellow,' said Omar Khayyam with misgiving to the Mouse.

'He has a will of iron!' agreed the Mouse loyally.

They all proceeded to the house of Sulkpot Ben Nagnag,

where Abu Ali turned to the other three and said: 'Well, my friends, here we part company for the time being.'

'Aren't we coming in with you?' asked the Mouse uneasily.

'No,' said Abu Ali kindly. 'You two must stay with Omar Khayyam.'

'But I hardly know him!' protested the Mouse. 'For all I know, he may keep a cat!'

'You may rely on me to protect you from *all* hostile carnivores, ma'am!' Omar Khayyam reassured her.

'Why, thank you!' said the Mouse, but added to Abu Ali: 'All the same, I shan't rest till I know you're safe!'

'Me neither!' agreed Boomalakka Wee unhappily.

'If all goes well, I'll send word to you within the hour,' Abu Ali promised them, knocking on the gate.

'And if all *doesn't* go well?' asked the Mouse.

'Never trouble trouble till trouble troubles *you*!' said Abu Ali. 'But just for safe-keeping,' he added, handing the Lamp to Omar Khayyam, 'I'll leave this in *your* care.'

'It couldn't be in safer hands,' Omar Khayyam assured him, slipping it absent-mindedly into his pocket.

At this moment, the gate opened.

'Oh, it's *you*, is it?' exclaimed the gateman, recognizing Abu Ali at once. 'Come *in*, my fine young gent! Sulkpot will be tickled *pink* to see *you* again!'

As soon as Abu Ali stepped inside, the guard slammed the gate behind him and locked it.

Omar Khayyam shook his head.

'That was *not* a hero's welcome!' he said uneasily.

'I *knew* we should have gone with him!' said the Mouse in bitter self-reproach.

'Well, all you can do now is obey his orders,' said Omar Khayyam. 'Would you care to ride home in my hat, ma'am?'

'Good Heavens, why? I have four perfectly good legs!' replied the Mouse sedately.

Meanwhile the guard led Abu Ali to where the Captain

of the Guard and Kublai Snoo were playing darts. When they saw Abu Ali, they gazed at him with open mouths.

'You don't mean to say you've come *back*?' demanded the Captain of the Guard incredulously. 'Why, you must be out of your *mind*, young fellamelad!'

'Yes, indeed!' agreed Kublai Snoo. '*You* didn't know when you were lucky!'

'Will you inform Sulkpot Ben Nagnag of my presence here?' Abu Ali requested politely.

'That's *exactly* what we'll do; and you'll come along and watch us!' said the Captain of the Guard, putting the point of his sword against Abu Ali's ribs and leading him into the house. 'Upon my word, I feel downright sorry for you!'

'I do too!' agreed Kublai Snoo. 'Old Nagnag hates you to pieces; cross my heart and hope to die! He does; doesn't he, Captain of the Guard?'

'That's for *us* to know, and *him* to find out!' said the Captain of the Guard ominously, and opened a door. 'In you go!'

In Abu Ali went, and there was Sulkpot Ben Nagnag lolling on a couch with his slippers off, playing with a little wire puzzle; and when he saw Abu Ali, he dropped the little wire puzzle and he sat bolt upright.

'WHAT? YOU AGAIN?' he shouted in capital letters, shuffling into his slippers. 'My eyes deceive me! What in the name of grumbling thunder induced you to come back here, you brazen-faced insect? Explain yourself INSTANTLY!'

'I found the Three Tail Feathers of the Magic Phoenix Bird,' Abu Ali informed him. 'And in view of the fact that the Wicked Princes only found *one* Magic Carpet, I claim the hand of Silver Bud!'

'You – *what*?' gasped Sulkpot, unutterably beside himself. 'You – you – you – *what*? I shall choke or something! Water, water! You have the *insolence* – you have the *audacity* – you have the *arrogance* to ask for the hand of my – of my –!'

Here he *did* choke, and fell hurriedly backwards on to the couch.

'Didn't I tell one of you dummies to bring me a drink of water?' he added hoarsely to the Captain and Kublai Snoo. 'Don't gape at me! I did! Where is it?'

'We can't leave the prisoner to go running off after glasses of water,' said the Captain of the Guard sulkily. 'He'd escape or something.'

'Oh, no, he wouldn't,' said Kublai Snoo with quiet calm.

'Oh, yes, he would,' said the Captain sharply.

'He wouldn't!' said Kublai Snoo swiftly.

'SILENCE!' roared Sulkpot Ben Nagnag, making a genuine effort to pull himself together. 'Now,' he said in a steadier voice, 'we'll deal with the situation in a cool, calm, and collected manner; if it's all the same to everybody! You, creature! You say you have the Three Tail Feathers from the Magic Phoenix Bird?'

'I do,' said Abu Ali.

'Then produce them!' barked Sulkpot.

'He *would* have escaped,' muttered the Captain under his breath.

'Oh, no, he wouldn't!' murmured Kublai Snoo, quick as a flash.

'WILL YOU BE QUIET!' roared Sulkpot, turning turkey purple. 'Do you understand me? Was I audible enough? BE QUIET!' He regained his breath with considerable difficulty, and turned to Abu Ali. 'I'm asking for the Three Tail Feathers!' he said darkly. 'Produce them!'

'I can't yet!' said Abu Ali. 'They were stolen by the Wicked Princes; so you'll have to wait till they get here.'

'You must take me for a doddering old idiot if you expect me to believe *that*!' snarled Sulkpot.

'*Would!*' said the Captain inaudibly.

'*Wouldn't!*' countered Kublai Snoo out of the corner of his mouth.

'*Look!*' said Sulkpot in an alarmingly hoarse whisper. 'The next sound *either* of you makes, you'll *both* go straight into the boiling oil! Is that absolutely clear?'

'Yes,' said the Captain of the Guard.

'No,' said Kublai Snoo.

'WHAT?' roared Nagnag, clutching at the couch.

'He can't throw us in the oil vat,' said Kublai Snoo to the Captain serenely. 'It's our afternoon off in a minute. We caught a suitor!'

'So we did! Where are you going?' asked the Captain of the Guard interestedly.

'Oh, just up and down the town,' said Kublai Snoo airily. 'Just looking about, and talking to people.'

'Would you mind if I came with you?' asked the Captain, charmed by the idea.

'Yes, if you like,' said Kublai Snoo generously. 'Have you any money?'

'A little,' admitted the Captain.

'Then we might go for a camel ride or something,' said Kublai Snoo. 'You can get a special return ticket which works out *very* reasonable.'

Abu Ali nudged them both, which was easy enough to do, as they were chatting across him; and the Captain of the Guard and Kublai Snoo jumped hastily to attention.

[92]

Sulkpot Ben Nagnag, who had been significantly tapping one foot, coughed.

'Quite finished?' he asked.

'Yes, thank you,' said the Captain.

'I *can* get a word in edgeways now?' inquired Sulkpot, deceptively polite.

'Yes, indeed!' said Kublai Snoo generously.

'*Thank* you!' said Sulkpot with heavy sarcasm.

'Thank *you*,' returned Kublai Snoo. 'And I'd like to add that I've always been very happy here.'

'Me too,' said the Captain of the Guard.

'Would you allow me a word, gentlemen?' asked Abu Ali, hoping to avert a scene.

'Be my guest!' said the Captain hospitably.

'Thank you,' said Abu Ali, addressing Sulkpot next. 'Permit me to remind you, sir, that I came here in good faith. I have told you the truth. The least I am entitled to, in return, is a fair hearing!'

'My, you *are* brave!' said Kublai Snoo admiringly.

'Don't worry! You'll get a fair hearing!' smouldered Sulkpot. 'As soon as the Princes arrive; so they can be used as evidence against you! Guards! Lock this insect in solitary confinement!'

'Is he allowed visitors?' asked the Captain.

'NO, YOU MUTTON HEAD, OF COURSE NOT!' yelled Sulkpot.

'Well; we were only asking,' said Kublai Snoo. 'Why are you always such a pig to us?'

Sulkpot drew himself to his full height.

'Both Guards! One pace forward march!' he ordered.

Kublai Snoo and the Captain beamed and marched one pace forward smartly, expecting promotion or at least a medal.

Sulkpot stretched out both his arms and banged their helmets together.

'*Ouch!*' cried the Captain.

'*Clang!*' cried Kublai Snoo.

'Now mark my every word!' said Sulkpot through tightly clenched teeth. 'If this prisoner escapes again, I'll boil all *three* of you in oil! Now bind the knave!'

The Captain and Kublai Snoo clapped hand-irons on Abu Ali's wrists.

'Now to the nethermost dungeon with him!' bellowed Sulkpot.

'Yes, sir! Right away, sir!' said the Captain. 'Prisoner! About face! Eyes right! Number off!'

'Not till I've said my say!' cried Abu Ali, really annoyed for the first time. 'I see now how rash I was to expect fair play! But as I still wish to win the love of Silver Bud *on my own merits alone*, I advise you to invite the Emperor of China to be present at my untimely end!'

'Well, we may not be able to manage *that*,' said Sulkpot sarcastically, 'but we'll send him a postcard afterwards! *Away* with him, Guards!'

Thus were the Mouse's profoundest fears fulfilled. Abu Ali was marched to the nethermost dungeon and given into the custody of a custodian so crude, coarse, and uncouth that he had been known to steal milk from blind kittens and eat soup off his knife.

This grisly gloombag locked Abu Ali in the deepest, darkest, dampest dungeon of them all, with only a sawn-off stool to sit on.

No sooner had this dastardly deed been done, than such a cacophonous commotion arose in the courtyard above that it even brought Silver Bud to the window of the room she was locked in.

To her misgiving, alarm, and dismay, she watched the Wicked Princes dismount from their caravans, to be warmly greeted by Sulkpot Ben Nagnag.

Chapter The Eleventh

Which Explains How Abu Ali, Greatly Helped by Loyal Friends, Was Nearly Able to Win the Day

You may well have wondered, gentle reader, how Silver Bud had fared during Abu Ali's absence, and I cannot paint a carefree picture for you, though her faith in Abu Ali never faltered for a moment. Indeed, her first reaction to the hullaballoo in the courtyard was one of hope that Abu Ali had at last returned; and only when she realized it was the Wicked Princes did the joy vanish from her face, and she turned away from the window, a prey to even deeper foreboding than before.

Indeed, what an appalling predicament yawned before her! Unless Abu Ali appeared more or less on the instant, Sulkpot would wed her to whichever Wicked Prince had brought back a Magic Carpet!

Little wonder that despair all but overwhelmed her!

All too soon, the door of her apartment was unlocked from the outside, and Sulkpot Ben Nagnag ushered in the Wicked Princes Tintac Ping Foo and Rubdub Ben Thud.

They were carrying the Magic Carpet and the Tail Feathers between them, and they looked as insufferable as ever.

'All hail to thee, fair Silver Bud!' brayed Rubdub. 'We return triumphant, as you can see! Here is the last Magic Carpet in the world!'

'It flies like a bird!' crowed Tintac Ping Foo. 'You have only to state your destination (provided your weight is normal), and you're there in a flash!'

'And these,' cried Rubdub, 'are the Tail Feathers of the extinct Phoenix Bird!'

'In short, Daughter,' preened Sulkpot, 'your suitors have fulfilled Abu Ali's task *as well as* their own! Therefore you shall choose between the Carpet and the Feathers, without knowing who brought which! Choose child!'

'I shall make *no* decision until Abu Ali returns!' returned Silver Bud resolutely, and to show that the subject was now closed, she walked proudly to the far corner of the room.

Ping Foo winked at Rubdub, and then at Sulkpot (who was in on it too), and then coughed.

'Dear Lady. Alas. This gives me great pain,' he said in a very sorrowful voice. 'I regret to inform you that Abu Ali was eaten by Dragons last Tuesday. We were there, Ben Thud and me, and saw it all.'

'R.I.P.,' said Rubdub, pretending to flick a tear from his eye.

'P.T.O.,' said Ping Foo.

'R.S.V.P.,' said Rubdub.

'M.Y.O.B.,' said Ping Foo.

'Indeed? Well, well! Too bad!' said Sulkpot insincerely. 'He was a fine figure of a lad!'

'We'll never see his like!' agreed Ping Foo.

'Still; life must go on!' said Sulkpot.

'Yes, yes!' said Rubdub. 'Laugh and the world laughs with you; snore and you sleep alone!'

'Which of us conquering heroes do you fancy, ma'am?' asked Ping Foo bewitchingly.

'Neither!' said Silver Bud coldly.

'*What?*' exclaimed Tintac Ping Foo in genuine surprise. 'Why not?'

'Because I don't believe you!' answered Silver Bud. 'And you have a nose like a hockey puck!'

'You are beside yourself!' cried Sulkpot hastily, for Ping Foo had clutched his nose protectively and gone very red. 'Come, gentlemen! Don't attach too much importance to this trivial tantrum! She'll come to her senses soon enough!'

Whereupon he stamped out with the Wicked Princes, banging and locking the door behind him.

Below in the dungeon, meanwhile, Abu Ali was sitting on the sawn-off stool wondering what he could use to dig a hole in the wall and thus escape, when suddenly the straw at his feet began to rustle, and the next moment the Mouse popped her head out and hissed: '*Hist!*'

'Mouse!' cried Abu Ali, overjoyed. '*How* did you get *here*?'

'Boomalakka Wee and Omar Khayyam and I decided that things must have gone awry. Which indeed they *have*!' she answered. 'So a mouse I met at Omar Khayyam's house was considerate enough to introduce me to the Prison Mice, who are *most* civil. Oh, by the way, Omar Khayyam said to tell you that if there's anything he can do, he'll be happy to oblige. Pointless of him, I thought, but he meant well. Your Three Tail Feathers arrived safely. They're up in Silver Bud's room at the moment, locked in with her. The Magic Carpet is there too.'

'Oh, *that* old thing,' answered Abu Ali without much thought, and then blinked and sat up. 'The Magic Carpet!'

he cried. 'Mouse! Go to Silver Bud and tell her to unroll the Magic Carpet in front of an open window, and we'll escape on it together!'

'But how will you ever get out of *here*?' asked the Mouse.

'I'll cross that bridge when I come to it,' said Abu Ali simply. 'Meanwhile, your place is at Silver Bud's side; she is now friendless and alone! Now off you go!' said Abu Ali.

'I'm proud of you!' cried the Mouse emotionally, as she burrowed back under the straw.

Left alone, Abu Ali hurried to the door and pressed his ear to the grille. Near by he could hear the Jailer eating an unripe turnip.

'Jailer!' he called.

'Wot?' growled the Jailer's voice from near by.

'A stone has just fallen out of the wall of my cell!' said Abu Ali.

'How big a stone?' asked the Jailer.

'It's as big as the hole,' answered Abu Ali.

'And how big is the hole?'

'I'm not sure. I haven't crawled through it yet,' replied Abu Ali. 'Shall I try?'

'No! Don't move till I get there!' shouted the Jailer, and the next moment a heavy old key rattled in the lock.

Abu Ali picked up a large clay water jug, and skipped behind the door. When it opened and the Jailer came in, he brought the jug down on the Jailer's head with all his might.

This would certainly have done the trick if the Jailer hadn't been wearing a helmet; but the Jailer was wearing a heavy brass helmet with a spike on top; and when the jug burst with a loud bang, it merely pushed his helmet a few inches nearer his nose. So he merely said: '*Wow!*' and pulled it straight again in plenty of time to see Abu Ali dashing out of the door; whereupon he instantly gave pursuit, bellowing: 'Stop him! Stop him!'

Abu Ali ran as fast as he could, but the Jailer kept close on his heels, and never stopped bellowing. Only a nose

ahead, Abu Ali whizzed round a corner of the passage, only to find himself heading *straight* towards five sentries who had heard the bellowing and were heading *straight* towards *him*.

Abu Ali stopped dead in his tracks and the Jailer pounced on him with a roar of triumph; but *just* as the Jailer pounced, Abu Ali dived under his legs, and the Jailer catapulted head-first into the sentries; and as the passage was not only narrow and dark but slippery, the Jailer and the sentries had *frightful* trouble distinguishing friend from foe.

This allowed Abu Ali to sprint along the passage until he reached the stone stairs that led to the entrance hall above.

He sprinted up the stairs two at a time; and he had *just* reached the top as a fresh contingent of guards came stumbling *down* them to investigate the trouble in the dungeons; and when they saw Abu Ali, they hurled themselves at him at the double.

By this time, the Jailer and the sentries had sorted themselves out enough to reach the bottom step of the stairs;

so Abu Ali found himself trapped fore and aft. Just as the Jailer and the sentries from below and the guards from above were about to converge on him, he suddenly noticed a Large Brass Lamp hanging from a chain to the ceiling of the entrance hall, so he *leaped* into the air and caught it.

By now the guards at the top of the stairs were running too fast to stop, so they collided head on with the Jailer and the sentries, who were only half-way up the stairs; and down they all rolled to the bottom. Abu Ali now swung on the Lamp until it was sailing backwards and forwards so fast that no one in his right senses would have dared to stop it.

The dungeons *and* the stairs *and* the entrance hall now *swarmed* with sentries and guards; and though Abu Ali was safe for the moment, he obviously couldn't spend the rest of his life swinging to and fro in mid-air.

Fortunately the Lamp was now sailing at such a speed that Abu Ali was able to aim himself at the front door and let go.

By the happiest of chances, the Wicked Princes Tintac Ping Foo and Rubdub Ben Thud chose this identical moment to come running into the house, so that Abu Ali's feet met Rubdub's tum and catapulted him backwards into Tintac Ping Foo; and Abu Ali was half-way across the courtyard before they realized what had hit them.

A creeper grew against the side of Sulkpot's house; and Abu Ali had scrambled up it by the time the guards had disentangled themselves from the Wicked Princes.

Silver Bud, hearing the hullaballoo below, ran to the window and looked out; and when she saw Abu Ali climbing into her window, she gave a little scream of excitement and tugged the Magic Carpet as near to the window as it would go.

'We must all keep calm and cool!' the Mouse kept twittering nervously.

'The key! The key!' screamed Sulkpot's voice outside the

door. 'I've lost the key! Break down the door, you block-heads! I shall choke or something! *Break it down!*'

Heavy blows at once began to shake the timber of the door.

'Hurry, Abu Ali! Hurry! They're breaking down the door!' called Silver Bud out of the window, and she and the Mouse pulled with all their might until Abu Ali tumbled into the room.

'Quick! On to the Carpet!' he cried, as the door began to splinter.

'Every man for himself!' encouraged the Mouse, leaping on to the Carpet first.

'To Peking in China, Carpet!' shouted Abu Ali, and just as the door fell in with a crash, the Carpet rose gracefully into the air and sailed towards the window.

Oh, reader; gentle reader! How can I bring myself to tell you? The window wasn't wide enough!

When the edges of the Carpet touched the sides of the window, the Carpet simply rippled to a halt and hung motionless in the air. The guards leaped up and caught it

by the edges, and easily brought it to the floor again.

Alas! Once more, poor Abu Ali was overpowered by superior force. They dragged him back to the dungeon in chains that were heavier than *he* was; and poor Silver Bud, locked in her room, was doomed to marry a Wicked Prince before the day was over.

Be that as it may, however, we must direct our attention elsewhere, where further complications were even now being set in motion.

Chapter The Twelfth

Which Brings the Story to Its Close

In his solitary cell, laden with a whole set of iron chains, Abu Ali prepared himself to face the worst.

And then, somewhere at the back of his mind, a thought suddenly stirred.

He sat straight up and frowned with concentration.

The thought became wide awake.

The Lamp!

What had Boomalakka Wee said? 'I can't get *back*. So Father can't get *here*!'

But since then, the spell had been *un*clogged by the Magician!

Abu Ali slapped his knees excitedly and leaped to his feet. All he had to do was to send a message to Omar Khayyam, telling him *first* to send Boomalakka Wee home, and *then* to rub the Lamp for Abdul, who would come roaring to the rescue!

Ah, but how to send the message?

At this imposing moment, there was a rap on the grille of his door, and when Abu Ali looked in that direction, he saw Kublai Snoo peering in from the other side.

'It's only me,' said Kublai Snoo shyly. 'It's my afternoon off. As you probably won't be here when we get back, I brought you this banana as a going-away present.'

He passed the banana graciously through the grille.

'How *very* kind of you,' said Abu Ali, touched.

'Oh, please! Think nothing of it!' said Kublai Snoo. 'Do you have a farewell message? I'll be glad to forward it to your next of kin!'

'*Will* you? How *doubly* kind of you!' exclaimed Abu Ali

gratefully. 'My next of kin is Omar Khayyam, in the Tent Shop near the Market Place. Would you ask him to rub the Lamp for Abdul? And would you repeat the message to me once, to make sure you have it right?'

'No, no, I'll remember this one!' promised Kublai Snoo. 'And the Captain's in a hurry for his camel ride! I must fly! Ta-ta!'

He vanished from the grille, leaving Abu Ali gravely doubting whether the message would reach Abdul *at all*, let alone in any condition to be of use.

Meanwhile, way off in his Tent Shop, Omar Khayyam had come to an historic decision.

'Anything's better than sitting here till we die of old age!' he rallied Boomalakka Wee. 'Let's go to Sulkpot's house and see what we can learn from the gate keeper!'

So off they went to Sulkpot's house, leaving the Lamp on the table of the Tent Shop.

As they crossed the Market Place, they passed Kublai Snoo and the Captain, who were on *their* way to Omar Khayyam's Tent Shop; but of course nobody recognized anybody, never having met.

Up in Silver Bud's apartment, the Mouse was in a quandary. Chancing to peer out of the window, she saw a *huge* contingent of guards marching towards the dungeons; and guessing the worst, she hurled herself into the hole in the wall and almost *dived* the whole way to Abu Ali's dungeon.

'Mouse, you're a mind-reader!' cried Abu Ali joyfully. 'I tried to send a message to Omar Khayyam to rub the Lamp for Abdul – but I'm *sure* it won't reach him in recognizable form!'

'Yes, it will! I will go myself!' cried the Mouse heroically. 'Meanwhile, use every trick in the book to delay the boiling!'

She had no sooner vanished under the pile of straw than the cell door was flung open, and in marched the *huge* contingent of guards.

They doubled the number of chains on his arms and legs, and then chained the arm-chains to the leg-chains; and a *particularly* mean-spirited guard even went so far as to snitch the banana.

The Mouse meanwhile had barely had time to scramble through the hole in Sulkpot's garden wall, when Omar Khayyam and Boomalakka Wee arrived at Sulkpot's front gate and banged on it loudly.

At the place of execution, the oil vats had already begun to bubble, and the Wicked Princes were being shown to V.I.P. front-row seats.

And *high* in the air, *far*, far away, the Magician began to detect trouble in the steering gear of the Land of Green Ginger.

He hastened to his book of spells and checked each one carefully; while the Land of Green Ginger began making such curious swerves that the lady Phoenix Bird toppled backwards into a stream, *insisting* to her husband that somebody had pushed her.

Meanwhile, the valiant Mouse went skipping through the crowded streets with a much better sense of direction than Boomalakka Wee; but even so, it was an exhausting ordeal.

Things had begun to worsen everywhere.

The gate keeper remembered Omar Khayyam from the time he had admitted Abu Ali, so he opened wide the gate; and as soon as they were inside, he yelled for the guards. So now Omar Khayyam and Boomalakka Wee were prisoners too.

And Abu Ali was brought to the place of execution, where the oil vats were now bubbling so ferociously that the reflected heat alone was being used for poaching ostrich eggs.

And Kublai Snoo and the Captain had *finally* found their way to Omar Khayyam's Tent Shop, and were banging on the door. As they very soon tired of *that*, the Captain lifted the latch and went in. Naturally they found nobody home, and they were *just* about to leave again when Kublai Snoo saw the Lamp.

'Oo! My old grannie had a lamp *exactly* like this one, only not so dirty!' said Kublai Snoo sentimentally. 'Cor, it *is* dirty, isn't it? I'll just give it a quick rub!'

'No, we'll be late for our camel ride,' objected the Captain; but his voice was drowned in a *terrible* clap of thunder, and the floor split open right under their noses.

Kublai Snoo was so terrified that he clutched the Captain around the neck; but as the Captain had clutched Kublai Snoo round the neck in equal terror, so they both fell to the floor with a thud as a *huge* Green Cloud bulged up into the room, and the awe-inspiring voice of Abdul boomed: 'I am the Slave of the Lamp! Ask what thou wilt and it shall be done!'

'Oh, please sir, don't eat us!' sobbed Kublai Snoo, unutterably beside himself. 'We promise never to do it again!'

'Do *what* again?' asked Abdul irritably. 'You must have needed me, or you wouldn't have rubbed the Lamp! What do you want?'

'We don't want *anything*!' cried Kublai Snoo in a panic. 'Oh, my goodness, I *wish* I'd never tried to help Abu Ali! I was *only* trying to be kind!'

'Abu Ali?' repeated Abdul swiftly. 'Where is he? If he's in trouble, woe betide his enemies!'

'Well, *we're* not his enemies!' quavered Kublai Snoo. 'We don't even *know* him! And even if we *did*, we wouldn't harm a hair of his head! *Please*, sir, can we go now?'

'Well, I suppose so!' said Abdul resentfully. 'But don't try and summon me again, after a false alarm like *this*!'

'No, no! We won't!' twittered Kublai Snoo.

At this moment, the Mouse staggered out of the wainscot, more dead than alive.

'No! No! Come back!' she squeaked to Abdul, just as he began to disappear.

'What? Again?' growled Abdul mutinously.

'*Eek! A mouse!*' shrilled the Captain, leaping on to a chair.

'You *are* Abdul, aren't you?' the Mouse demanded urgently. 'Oh, kind sir; hurry to Sulkpot Ben Nagnag's house and rescue Abu Ali!'

Abdul – half Green Smoke and half highly inflammable Djinn – eyed her unsociably.

'First of all, I want to know who I'm to believe, and who I'm *not* to!' he warned her nastily. 'And let the clot beware, who lies to me!'

'Oh, Glory Ducketts; please *hurry*!' beseeched the Mouse. 'They're going to *boil* him in *oil*!'

'I don't move a *step* until I'm satisfied it's not another wild goose chase!' answered Abdul implacably. 'I'll take you first, miss! Do you have your credentials with you? If so, kindly produce them!'

Meanwhile at Sulkpot Ben Nagnag's house, the hour of execution had begun to strike.

Abu Ali stood on a trap-door over the boiling oil vat, still chained and bound; and near by stood Omar Khayyam and Boomalakka Wee, also chained and bound. The Wicked Princes had decided that they were to follow Abu Ali into the oil vat as an encore.

May I digress here for a moment to suggest to you, gentle reader, that the real test of a true hero is not how boldly he behaves when all is going well, but how nobly he behaves when all seems lost?

Suppose, for example, *you* were standing in chains, on a trap-door over a vat of boiling oil. As a true hero, you would have to rise above your station, would you not? And show your detractors how a truly brave man can die.

This was, of course, the course to which Abu Ali intended to recourse.

Secretly, no doubt, he *might* have been regretting his refusal to make use of his Royal Title, now that it was too late to change horses in midstream. Secretly, no doubt, his heart *may* have been rending in twain at the thought of bidding farewell to Silver Bud.

Not a trace of it showed on his face.

This I find quite admirable, gentle reader. The will to win is always half the battle. We are only as brave as we think we are. While hope is not lost, nothing is lost.

'Wretch! It is time to say your last words!' bumbled Sulkpot. 'Keep them brief and to the point!'

'Can you give me the exact time at my disposal?' petitioned Abu Ali civilly. 'It will obviously dictate my choice of subject matter.'

'I'll give you exactly one minute!' answered Sulkpot.

'I'm sorry,' said Abu Ali, 'but if you'll try it yourself, you'll realize that one minute is too short.'

'Nonsense!' shouted Ping Foo rudely. 'I could compose a *superb* farewell address in one minute!'

'Then do it!' Abu Ali begged him cordially.

'I will!' cried Ping Foo. 'Ladies and gentlemen! It is a far, far better farewell address I give you than anything old Rubdub Ben Thud would be able to cook up! It is to a far, far better place I go, than the place they'll send old Rubdub! In the words of the dear old song: *I don't want to lose me, but I know I have to go –'*

'Time! Your minute's up!' shouted Rubdub loudly. 'And they were *pretty* feeble last words; weren't they, Sulkpot?'

'They were, rather,' conceded Sulkpot, beginning to wonder why the execution was getting out of hand.

'Then it's only fair to let Ben Thud do better!' proposed Abu Ali.

'Hear, hear! Well said! Exactly!' shouted Rubdub with great pleasure. 'Gentlemen of the Jury –!'

'Speak *your own* last words, prisoner!' interrupted Sulkpot impatiently.

'Very well,' said Abu Ali. 'My last words are these! If one of those Princes were about to become *my* son-in-law, I'd *much* prefer Rubdub Ben Thud. He would steal *far* less of my wealth!'

'Why, thank you, thank you, Abu Ali!' cried Rubdub, *immensely* flattered. 'Oh, how nobly said! I shall see you get a truly *beautiful* tombstone!'

'Sir,' one of the guards called down to Sulkpot. 'The oil will soon be off the boil!'

'Then heat it up again, you blockhead!' scolded Sulkpot.

'I would if I could, but we've run out of wood,' said the guard apologetically.

'Then in he goes, ready or not!' bellowed Sulkpot. 'Release the trap-door!'

'Right!' called a guard, and pulled the lever. There was a loud blood-curdling creak, and then silence.

'Oh, oh,' said the guard in embarrassment, 'it's stuck, Boss! Won't be a jiffy!'

But as he began to tinker with the lever, a cry rang out.

'Who rang out that cry?' demanded Rubdub nervously.

'Master! Look at that up there!' Small Slave yelled in terrified accents, pointing to the sky.

Everyone craned their necks upwards, and then a *wave* of alarm spread through the assembly.

Zooming down towards them, like a great big wobbling wide-winged bird, was the Land of Green Ginger!

Oh, what chaos ensued! *Oh*, what panic and confusion! Everyone became as stupid as sheep and ran in several directions at the same time; and the Land of Green Ginger had no sooner settled down on top of them all with a *ker-foomph, ker-woompha, ker-woomp!* than a huge cloud of Green Smoke came rolling out of the boiling oil vat, and Abdul's indignant face appeared in the middle of it.

'Everybody, except for Abu Ali and friends, cease doing what you're doing; no matter *what* you're doing!' roared his angry voice; and *instantly* everybody except Abu Ali and friends was frozen into whatever undignified position he happened to be in at the moment.

As Abu Ali leap-frogged down from the trapdoor, the Magician came trotting through the Ginger Trees and Abdul came to rest on the ground. The Mouse at once poked her head out of his sash, coughing slightly from the Green Smoke.

'My dear Abu Ali; what an *energetic* life you lead!' the Magician exclaimed. 'Allow me to unchain you!'

'No, no! Allow *me*!' insisted Abdul, making a pass in the air with his hands. The chains at once fell from Abu Ali with a resounding clatter.

'Silver Bud!' cried Abu Ali at once. 'I must go to her! Which way is the house?'

'I'll consult my compass,' promised the Magician; but there was no need. At that very same moment Silver Bud came running towards them through the Ginger Trees.

'Abu Ali! I don't understand what's happened to our garden; but I'm *so* glad you're safe!' she cried in delight, throwing herself into his open arms.

At this touching sight, the Magician and Abdul turned away discreetly and conversed with the Mouse; allowing Abu Ali to dry Silver Bud's tears and offer her a hundred other charming little attentions which are without importance except to those personally concerned.

And all this time, gentle reader, Sulkpot and the Wicked Princes and the guards remained frozen into decorative ornaments – though I use the word decorative in its *loosest* sense. None of you, for instance, would win a prize if you had Rubdub Ben Thud crowding up your front hall with the evening paper tucked under his arm; besides which, his ridiculous expression of anguish would upset your cat.

As for Tintac Ping Foo, even if you were to stick him up in a bean patch to scare birds, the puniest pewee would pooh-pooh him with impunity.

Abu Ali now presented Silver Bud to Abdul and the Magician, and she greeted them charmingly, not forgetting to express her gratitude for the timeliness of their combined rescue.

'But how,' Silver Bud asked Abdul, 'were you able to summon Boomalakka Wee, if only one of you can answer the Lamp at the same time?'

'Come, come, my dear,' said Abdul tolerantly. 'It is far too near the end of the story for scientific explanations!'

'Oh dear, *look* at poor Papa!' cried Silver Bud, noticing Sulkpot for the first time. '*And* the Wicked Princes! *And* all the guards! Are they in pain?'

'No, no, my love,' Abu Ali consoled her. 'They're perfectly comfortable; and they'll only stay like that till we depart for Peking.'

'For Peking?' asked Silver Bud in understandable surprise. 'Why Peking?'

'Because,' said the Mouse, bursting with pride at being the bearer of such impressive tidings, 'Abu Ali is none other than Prince Abu Ali of China!'

'My goodness!' exclaimed Omar Khayyam. 'He told me that long ago, and I took it for a whopper!'

[113]

'*I* knew it all the time!' boasted Boomalakka Wee; which *was* only boasting; but he was so anxious to appear right about *something* for once that no one had the heart to contradict him.

'Why *ever* didn't you tell my father who you really were?' Silver Bud asked Abu Ali in innocent amazement.

'Because I mightn't have impressed you *half* as much, dear Silver Bud,' said Abu Ali, 'if I'd swaggered in here in my royal robes, ordering everybody to bow and scrape to me!'

'For shame! You'd have impressed me *exactly* as you did, no matter *how* you'd come here!' Silver Bud reproved him.

Abu Ali was much too intelligent to make a mountain out of such a molehill.

'What's done is done, and no bones are broken,' he pointed out tactfully. 'And we do at least possess Three Feathers which we could have obtained no other way!'

'We do indeed!' agreed Silver Bud contentedly. 'Even if we never find a practical use for them!'

'They would make a superlative nest!' hinted the Mouse acquisitively.

'Then they're yours!' said Silver Bud generously.

The Magician and Abdul now rejoined them.

'And now where would you and your charming bride like to go next, Abu Ali?' asked the Magician.

'To the Imperial Palace in Peking, if you please!' said Abu Ali.

'Take your seats, and *away* we go!' chirruped the Magician, and the very next moment the Land of Green Ginger lifted lightly off the house of Sulkpot Ben Nagnag and skimmed away into the wide blue yonder.

I hardly need assure you that Silver Bud made Abu Ali the most delectable of wives and later the most indispensable of Empresses; and you will be glad to hear that the Mouse took up permanent residence as the governess of their progeny.

I dearly wish I could add that she was eventually reconciled with her friend who had run away to sea; but even in tales such as this, not *everything* can end happily. The fate of the friend remains an inscrutable equation, and she remained a spinster to the end of her long and industrious life.

And that, patient and forbearing reader (to whom it has been a pleasure to address myself), is the Wonderful Tale of the Land of Green Ginger.